KEEPING THE EDGE

AN ANTHOLOGY OF
NEW URBAN FICTION

Keeping The Edge

Editors: Alex Poppe, Tony Clerkson
Cover design: Stephen Cameron
Cover photography: Tony Clerkson
Typesetting: Tony Clerkson

ISBN-13: 978-1497571099
ISBN-10: 149757109X

CONTENTS

i

BREAK
by Syd Briscoe

knock knock
Knock **KNOCK**
BANG
BANG

'*Whit* the fuck
are you doing?'

'Why won't
you answer my
calls? I've been
ringing you for
weeks!'

'For fuck's sake.'

'Don't shut that
fucking door!'

1

'D'you wannae keep your voice down? You're gonna wake the whole building up.'

'I just want you to answer my questions.'

'So phone me.'

'You won't answer! It's been twelve years, I just want you to answer my questions!'

'Just let it go, will you?'

'It's been twelve years, you owe me that much!'

'What the fuck's going on?'

'Oh, so she's here.'

'I said let it go.'

'What are you doing here? He doesn't want to talk to you.'

'It's none of your fucking business!'

'Don't talk to her like that.'

'I'll talk to her however I want! Why won't you answer my questions?'

'I'm phoning the police.'

'Good! Have
fun being
arrested for
bigamy!'

'It was annulled,
you mad bitch.'

'God
doesn't give
annulments!'

*'Why can't
you just
leave us
alone?'*

'Don't even try.
She's mental.'

'I'm not
mental! It's
been twelve
years! You'll get
yours!'

'Just fucking get out before you get yourself arrested!'

'We haven't done anything wrong, Melanie.'

'You're both going to hell! Enjoy burning together!'

'Get out! Fucking leave!'

'Shouting at her isn't helping.'

'Don't you dare try and defend me!'

SLAM

CRACK

'Oh my God!'

'You broke
my foot,
you bastard!'

'Shouldnae
have put it in
the fucking
door then.'

'You're both
going to hell!'

'Just get out!
Fucking limp
home!'

*'The police are on
their way.'*

'Just get the
fuck out! Leave
us alone!'

'Please just go.'

'Fuck off and
leave us alone!'

STOMP
STOMP

SLAM

STOMP

Stomp
stomp

THE END WILL BEGIN
by Ewan Morrison

He studies the wind: its speed, direction, what threat it carries within its scent. Five miles it is to the edge of the city though distances are no longer measured in miles per hour but in energy per risk. He steps through broken glass, checking abandoned cars for remnants overlooked, for petrol caps still intact, for fuel to hose-suck and billycan, but no opportunity. Hunger has finally forced him to leave his hideout and start his search for them. The sweet smell of burned plastic and purification hangs heavy as he skirts the shopping precincts shadows. Through alleys, he glimpses stores beyond. The mall is blackened caves now, fringed with shards, a multitude of melted plastics twisted into inhuman forms. Beneath his feet, ash covered, lie sunglasses, single sneakers, phones, computers still boxed, dresses on their hangers, price tags on all. In the first days they stole signifiers of status, no thought for value when the power grid ended. They starved then, staring at their blank screens.

No trace of food now, the stench of human waste on

every street, the survivors had moved out as he'd predicted they would. Every home has only enough food for three meals. What happens when the supply chain is cut? He'd asked them such questions, trying to get them to think, to question.

He navigates corner shops stripped bare. In Poundstretcher the shelves have been broken to make a fire. He can read the signs now, like an Indian tracker; embers on the burnt lino, hair of cat. RS McColl's, WHSmith, Bargain Booze, Costcutter. His gaze and feet never linger; he scans for human movement and cans, his hand ready, always, on the blade handle. He told them, panic buying will clear out a superstore in less than four hours. They wouldn't listen.

He skirts a tower block, fire scorched upper floors, remains of those who jumped. He checks for shoes but they have already been taken. Plastic bags and paper money circle in the wind. Streets further out, from the window above Tesco hangs the body of a youth, head hooded. Graffiti on the wall proclaims the site as property of a militia. He hides behind a car, moves on swiftly, blade unsheathed. Still no living soul. No police or military now. It was as he predicted; they too would abandon their posts. They had families to feed.

He nibbles the last crust, saving half.

Beneath the silent flyover he passes a near-naked woman, forty feet high. The lower part of her belly has been torn away leaving it without slogan or product. She smiles out over a hundred abandoned cars like some deceitful deity to him alone. Her eyes say, 'Why did so few of you read the signs?' 'I did,' he replies, 'but no one listened.'

A clatter and some footfall behind him. He jumps, the blade primed above his head. He locates an old man pushing a shopping trolley across the road. It has a broken wheel and the man is shoeless. Inside the trolley are what seem to be rags and wires. The old man does not seem to have noticed him. He stops by a bus shelter and sits on the seats. He looks down the road as if waiting for a bus.

He walks outer streets now – circles, suburbs, signs for neighbourhood watch schemes. For some reason he cannot fathom, pages blow here: a hundred thousand, images and words, newspapers, magazines, flying, falling, lying over cars, gardens, walls. That same old female smile, the seductive curves of advertising, the same dead words of news that was not the true news.

He had thought to maybe rest, but here it is worse than the centre. Bungalow after bungalow, it is as if each has vomited its contents. Among the garden gnomes, CDs, clothes, lightbulbs, cushions, socks and photos, insects swarm around forms that seem to be clothes laid out in human shapes. Among a child's toys and scattered books, a woman's legs are mould blue, the belly bloated, the crotch a bloodied brown. The bodies increase in number as the affluence grows. In the suburbs things have moved beyond the search for food. Desperate rituals have been enacted as if some primal revenge was long overdue. An entire family – mother, father and three children – are dead inside their SUV, propped up, sunglasses on, their bodies obviously arranged for some joke, or photo. Beds and chairs have been stacked and burned in a bonfire on the centre of a roundabout. The spikes of a picket fence display an array of human heads, leathered skin pulled tight into rictus grins.

It is the sleeplessness that causes the madness. He knows this, had warned of this. More than the lack of water and food, after four days with no sleep, you become paranoid, primordial. You watch your back, you smell enemy, you strike first, become a killer. Democracy will not survive beyond the seventh day, and they laughed. She did.

All of the doors in this crescent are kicked in. Inside a kitchen, he pulls out all the drawers. He finds a knife behind the fridge, some paracetamol. He had wanted to stop, rest for a while, but the gangs have left their faeces on the floor, territorial markings.

There are pictures on the wall still, of what must have been the family, and this must be a sign for him to keep on.

The motorway would be safer now, he tells himself, but takes no risks. He crawls then runs along the edges of fences and hedges. Uses his binoculars. The motorway is like some old black and white photo, time frozen. For four hundred yards in either direction the cars stand still and empty, some pushed to the side, or lying on their sides, broken glass reflecting the now setting sun. Torn clothing in the wind, birds circling.

And he had told them till he was dry of mouth – people will stay in their cars queuing for petrol till their own engines run dry. They'll block the roads for the very petrol tankers and food containers they're waiting for. They won't believe that the government can't help them, that the corporations can't provide for them, that their money is worthless. Like spoiled kids they'll huff in their cars, thinking them private property, thinking petroleum to be their birth right.

When he finds them, this time there will be no need for explanation.

Two hundred yards on, a swathe has been cut through the abandoned cars, by a lorry or tank; he cannot tell. He follows its corridor of wreckage. At the final junction a military vehicle with caterpillar tracks lies overturned. He had told them the gangs would overwhelm the soldiers, steal their weapons, pillage and rape at gunpoint, exhaust the cities and then start on the countryside.

His feet do not ache. He has long since taught himself to cut off pain at its root.

Sound of an engine. He throws himself down, shards cutting his bandaged hands. He belly creeps under a car, listens, waits; crawls beneath a truck, listens, waits; breathes, nothing. He makes it to the edge and jumps the small wall, cowering then bolting as if under fire.

Breathless now, overlooking from a ridge, he registers no movement below. He waits, checks. Rumours of ash, dust cloud and bird, nothing more. The petrified cars extend to the east and the hills, to the west and the sea.

The fools had all tried to evacuate at the same time and so destroyed one another's chances. The hillside around him is strewn with suitcases, rucksacks, toys, bottles. He pictures families fleeing the gangs, falling. It may be the numbers of the cars or the dead they imply or the thought of the long search ahead and the fading light and its crayon colours, but his eye wets now, for the first time since day one.

He would not kill himself as so many had done. He would force himself to survive, and this was not a matter of pride. He did not pay much heed to this wasted body now. He cared only for one thing: his children. He would follow the trail of the evacuees and find them. If he did not, the method of his departure had been well rehearsed, practiced on beasts – the knife, stone sharpened, in one deep slash, severing the jugular, the vocal chords, the windpipe, piercing the cartilage to the nerves of the cervical spine.

Sometimes sunset, sometimes the knife, sometimes not, but always the motorway and the children, this was the image that haunted Ed through the nights and hours of the day whenever thought strayed free. Lucid dream or obsessive delusion, he did not care for his shrink's diagnosis. It would come to him while watching his laptop start up, walking home from Sainsbury's with shopping bags, filling up his Volvo, buying a scratch card, channel hopping or queuing at the self-service checkout counter at Tesco.

'Are you collecting kids for sport vouchers?' the girl would ask.

'If only you knew,' was the thought. 'All of you...' Followed by, as if it were the necessary second note in a melody '...how all of this will end.'

He was drawn to spaces of transit, car parks, underpasses and overpasses at night. Alone, always, standing at the railings with his shopping bags, headphones on listening to Mahler, watching the miles of cars streaming into the night beneath his feet.

'There will be no more streetlights,' 'No more MP3s,' 'No more music.' White lights oncoming, red receding. Taking the headphones out to hear the wall of all that sound, to feel the weight of mass metal moving nowhere.

'There will be no more cars,' 'no more radio stations,' 'no more news bulletins.'

The immensity of their collective delusion. Some secret force filled his hollow. Some power, infinite, and expanding, took his breath, chocked him with tears. Beauty was the only word he had for it, an aesthetic and ethical perfection, like the finale in an opera had to be the summation of all its themes, like a well calculated equation could have only one inevitable conclusion.

'There will be no more adverts for things.' 'No more new things.'

The power of this truth revealed to him alone.

'Everything here will be the last of its kind.'

Weeping in his car in the car park between Toys'R'Us and Burger King, at the sight of families stuffing their branded boxes into their SUV's, their children, faces smeared with ketchup, with ice-cream, screaming for more.

'There will be no more toys,' 'No more credit cards or credit,' 'There will be no more petrol,' 'No more ice-cream.'

In the fresh dairy produce aisles in Sainsbury's, staring at a couple of students trying to decide on whether they'd have Dolcelatte or Brie or Lo Fat Yankee Cheese Dip or Reduced Fat French Stilton or Spanish Manchego.

'There will be no more foreign countries,' 'There will be no choice.'

On the train to work, watching the young people, so attractive, but all, each of them, sixty in the carriage, on their smartphones, gazing at their screens, texting, playing, watching, avoiding all eye contact with each other.

'There will be no more signal,' 'No more games,' 'No more memory cards.'

Standing by the edge of the train platform, closing his eyes as the express tore the air from his lungs.

'No more power lines,' 'No more timetables,' 'No more time.'

Watching a solitary old lady in a tartan shawl religiously place her empty bottles into the recycling bins, hesitating on where to put a brown one.

'There will be no more 'doing your little bit for the planet,' 'No more charity.'

And the words then, like a voice harmonising with the first, 'It's too late to do anything for these people,' 'It's too late to even tell them the truth,' 'Why save them? They'd only be competitors for the last remaining resources.'

Stuck in traffic on the expressway, he would close his eyes and picture the cars stopping, the noise starting, the fights breaking out. The panic buying of petrol. Day One, Day Two, Day Three. The thousands of abandoned cars on the motorway. He was studying the collapse of different civilisations, the patterns, the over-complexity that leads to structural weakness.

He mapped it out. He studied economics. Sixty-seven trillion dollars of debt in the shadow banking system, circling the planet, waiting to fall to earth with the gravity of a meteor strike. It would start with an economic crash initiated by China refusing to buy more American debt; the dollar and the euro would collapse. The savings of everyone in the developed world would vanish. Hyperinflation of eight hundred to one thousand percent. The system of international trade would collapse. OPEC would stop the flow of its oil. Billions of tons of food would be stuck at ports. Oil, the glorious interdependence of the global economy, would be revealed as its Achilles' heel; no country was self-sufficient, no nation would be spared, wars for resources would consume all resources, entire populations would starve.

He began studying human behaviour in times of crisis. He studied Hurricane Katrina, the economic collapse in Cyprus, the LA riots, the New York blackout. After three days with no food civilians turn to looting. After four to rioting. By the seventh day armed gangs and militias loot, rape and pillage. The facts were identical internationally.

In the past these things had been stopped before escalation became irreversible by the intervention of the state or foreign powers, but there would be no one to come and help when the collapse hit everybody.

He set up a blog called SURVIVAL.COM, to connect with other survivalists, to share info and flags and tipping points. He set up a programme to map fluctuations in the DOW and FTSE and studied Self-Reinforcing Positive Feedback Loops. All of his graphs pointed to the same thing; all headed upwards in almost vertical lines to a coming singularity within the next three to four years.

He wrote: *In 4000 BC the population was one billion and it stayed that way with only minor fluctuations till 1800 AD. One billion is the planet's natural equilibrium. The population of the world is now seven billion. The massive growth was a result of the emergence of complex systems for producing and distributing food, fuel, medicine, energy and raw materials within a rapidly globalising world economy. When the crash hits, the world will revert to the condition it was pre-1800. These systems are too complex to survive. Six billion people will be surplus to requirements. They will die.*

He wrote: *When you accept what will come to pass, you will go through stages of emotional readjustment comparable to that experienced after the loss of a loved one. Something has died in your heart and mind – the world as it was. You will go through denial, you will feel violent rage, you will try to bargain with the future, you will be so depressed you cannot move, you will face suicide and then, only then, will you accept. I have been through these states and survived. I intend to survive with my family through what is to come.*

He wrote: **It is better to be one year too early than one day too late.**

He became convinced that those in power were sending coded signals to one another, digging bunkers, performing test evacuations. Why else would so many movies contain the same damn image that haunted his head? Whether the crisis be zombies or planet collision or plagues or aliens, there was always a deserted highway and one man struggling along with a child in his arms.

There was just one problem. One that became increasingly inviolable the more he prepared and monitored fluctuations in the Dow and FTSE, the more he mapped escape routes and planned then fitted-out the place where he would hide his children: Justine.

Justine the just, the self-righteous, petty-minded, power-dressing, snooty-nosed, health-food addicted, high-heeled, home-shopper. Justine his ex-wife, who had hospitalised him, who had fought for and won full custody of his children, who had granted him 'access' only on her terms. Every time he tried to picture himself explaining politics to her, he got flashbacks of her first reactions, the year before.

'You've been watching too many horror films! I hope you haven't let Benjamin watch them too.' She'd laugh. He wouldn't be able to meet her eye. 'Are you still taking your anti-depressants? You know coming off them too quickly can be dangerous.'

Justine was a problem. And in truth, actually, so were his own kids.

He could picture Ella. He would say to her. 'Darling, it's started. We have to go and hide now.' She wouldn't even look up, her eyes stuck to her smartphone 'Aw dad, do we have to do this shit today – I'm meeting Suze and Jay and Saz at Abercrombie at three!' 'Aw Dad, drop me off at the mall, please, please, pretty pretty please with sugar on top. If you don't, Mom'll have to do it and she'll be so pissed at you.' 'Hey, maybes we could do your apocalypse shit next week. I'd deffo be up for that. That'd be well beast.'

There would be no more malls, no more Abercrombie, no more shopping. No, but there would also be no more Ella and no more Ben if he couldn't find a way to save them from themselves and from their mother.

He has time, a little, to perfect his plan. He will harden himself. He starts counting the days till the end will begin.

THE WEE MAN
by Lynsey Calderwood

On the bus pished and dying fur a pish, so he was, the wee man. He'd been oot since fucking twelve bells the day before and that was him just heading up the road.

Anyway there he was, fucking nearly doubled right ower and they'd hardly went past the Citizens' Theatre. So he knew that was it – fucking rank-a-dank time – he knew he was gaunae have tae go right there cause there was nae way he was gaunae make it aw the way tae Birgidale Road. Naw, nae fucking chance ae that, man.

So basically, what he did was he got up and walked right tae the back ae the bus. Fucking right up tae the gods where aw the wee twelve and thirteen-yir-auld diddies usually sit wi their cargos. Noo, there was nae cunt sitting up there by the way, nae cunt at aw. Cause he's had a right good swatch tae check in case there was, in case there was weans or that cooried doon underneath the seats. Cause obviously he didnae want tae just whip it oot an risk pure offendin folk. I mean, he's wisnae a fucking dirty bastart awthegether. He was trying tae be discreet aboot it. And the whole time he was walking up there he's aw pure paranoid especially when he saw this lassie he recognised –

Fucking hinging looking bitch wi a face like an infested fanny – that he made the mistake ae shagging aboot a month ago.

Anyway, it was just hard lines there wasnae a Barr Bru or a Bucky bottle or something lying aboot cause that would have made the job that bit tidier. Usually at that time ae night there's loadsa empties wedged between the seats.

He had another wee look aboot himsel anyway, just tae be on the safe side. The last thing he needed was some wee eighty yir auld granny wi a Sony Ericsson keeking oot at him, fucking phoning up the body poppers and getting him done for indecent exposure.

Cause he could just imagine it up in court, fucking Judge McGudge gaun like that tae him:

'And why, Mr Campbell, did you shake your penis in Mavis McShoogle's face?'

'Well your honour, you see, I was just trying tae get rid of the last few drops of pish…'

Next thing he knows, he's got six months in Barlinnie and he's on the fucking paedo register and banned fae seeing his wean. Aye right!

Fucking fanny face spotted him at that point and was pure heavy looking him up and doon. He wasnae sure what her problem was. Pure skanky weirdo. It wasnae like he'd done anything bad tae the lassie: it wasnae like he'd just done her and left. Naw, it wasnae like that. He had manners. He'd waited a good hauf an hour after he'd finished, and even attempted small talk before telling her he was working the next day and had tae be up early bells. She knew the score, anyway. Two fucking consenting adults that's what they were. And he never wanst said he'd phone her or wanted tae see her again.

Cause see the wee man, he might be a lot ae things; he might take a good bevy; and, aye, he'd been in clink; and he'd had a few fucking troubles in his time, but he wasnae a total arsehole.

He drew her heavy growlers right back and she turned away and said something tae her equally skanky pal.

He'd done nothing wrang. So he'd nothing tae feel bad aboot. And she was fucking lucky that she got her hole at aw. Cause nae danger would that have happened if he'd been sober.

Sake.

That was it.

He couldnae wait any longer, man.

He turned his back, did his zip, and started pishing away.

And what a pish it was!

Fuck, if there was a world championship fur it then he could surely pish for Scotland. He was having a rare tear tae hissel just thinking aboot it and what it would aw entail when he heard this voice:

'Here, fuck you daein looking at ma burd?'

He wisnae a hunner percent sure if it was aimed at him so he just ignored it and kept on pishing.

The voice got closer: 'I asked you a question, baldy baws,' it said. 'Fuck you daeing looking at my burd?'

He opened his mooth tae tell the guy tae fuck off, but he didnae get a chance cause FUCK YE the cunt got him by the back ae the neck and slammed him up against the bus windae, and was hauding him there wi his fucking sore fizzog squashed right up against the glass.

By this time the pish was gaun aw directions like a squinty Niagara fucking Falls. The wee man couldnae control it at aw and he could feel the wetness seeping into his jeans and his T-shirt, and it was warm against his belly.

Fucking humiliating. He was ready for greeting but the only thing that stopped him was the fear ae mair humiliation.

Finally, the guy let him go. He crumpled doon ontae the ground.

'You're a very fucking lucky boy,' said the guy. 'Next time you look at my burd I'll make you dae mair than pish yourself.'

He booted the wee man in the arse.

'Know what I'm saying ya knob end?'

The wee man grunted, pulled himself up using the yella bus pole.

He was never wan fur fighting, the wee man. But even though this cunt was a big barra ae a fella, he was sure he woulda been able tae haud his ain if he hadnae been hauding his cock.

He pressed the bell for the bus tae stop. His heid was

fucking lowpin, so it was, and he was seeing fucking stars and kaleidoscopic faces.

Everybody in the bus was watching, fucking laughing at him, specially fucking fanny face an her pal.

The guy was aboot tae walk away, but then the wee man shouted him back.

'Here, big man,' he said, 'is this yours?' and when the guy turned, he booted him in the baws and ran like fuck.

And he didnae look back either; he just kept running doon the gangway and aff the bus intae the night. And he kept on running till he was haufway doon his maw's street, and that's when he saw a police car pull up next tae him. And then he looked doon and thought FUCK! Cause he just realised that he still had his fucking cock out.

HOME
by Graeme Rae

It was the closing night of Black Bo's Bar. Management, eccentric rascals and recalcitrant to the end, had not installed a card machine, hung TV screens or decorated in twenty-four years. Layered old gig and Fringe posters going back to the eighties peeled from the black walls. The high ceiling was nicotine tan, the toilet free range and DJ Dolphin Boy – now forty-six and a father of three – was still spinning the same old ambient and nu-jazz *toons*. It was here that the best, the real conversations of Tom's life had taken place, and always with the same three friends – though wars, government, jobs, lovers came and went. Candle after candle had lit their thoughtful faces, angered faces, beaming, bored or ridiculous faces while they worked out in real time who they were, leaning in to the light to show they cared, as all the while rivers of wax engulfed the wine bottle.

In their usual dark corner beside the decks Tom sat staring at the usual round of drinks on the table. Opposite him a Trappist (untouched small bottle at table edge, shredded label) and then, clockwise, a Levitation (pint, half-empty, two rings of foam, centre table), his own Guinness (fourth since they'd all left, in his hand and still empty), the Argentinian Primitivo (barely touched, one perfect print of lipstick and a floating tobacco tendril, also centre table). Tonight, of all nights, they'd decided to announce their wedding. September, so everyone could arrange time off. Thoughtful. The gushed protestations and reassurances quickly began to sound hollow. They all knew the truth. Everything they'd been before tonight was over.

Tom started with the Primitivo.

Outside, Tom steadied himself against the bar's window ledge. His mind reeled and spun far, far away from the dull cold of the cobbled street. A group of people without proper edges materialised from a parallel universe and moved past him on a glistening ocean of bubble-wrap. In their own huddle they smoked and muttered, casting sideways glances in his direction.

'You wanna get yersel' home, mate!' one of them shouted through a black hole.

'Ain't no such place, my friend,' Tom hollered blindly. 'My jury! Everything's broken. You'll see. There's nowhere to make a stand. No... no flag to salute. Bro-ken!' He breathed in deeply a few times and little by little his head cleared. The bubble-wrap stopped surging.

Up on the High Street the queue had already formed. Those at the front would step inside a black car like the gondola of some gothic Ferris wheel. It would shoot off and another would immediately take its place. Tom decided to be audacious tonight. Once he'd pinballed right up to the front of the queue, he bundled himself straight through the first open door, closing it briskly behind him. A clamour erupted and several twisted faces loomed up at the glass, their fingers jabbing a warning.

'Home, thanks.' The driver's deadpan in the mirror reminded him to give his address.

As the taxi carried him off he sank back into his seat. In a passing shop doorway, silhouetted against lurid blue neon, a half-naked teenage girl bent double and vomited, her back arching as she convulsed. A laughing boy with jagged red hair winked at his mate and mimed thrusting his groin into her from behind. She straightened up, unsteady on high wedged heels, and wiped her mouth. The mate pulled out a bottle of something, held it high and they all punched the air. The derangement unleashed by booze seemed to be everywhere out there, even in the less obviously drunk. Gestures were a little too emphatic, gaits a little too self-conscious, laughter a little too theatrical and leers a little too careless. It was all too unreal and more like a symptom of some corrosive disorder. It seemed to Tom that behind all these faces something had been crushed or was calling out for help. He stared with the unblinking puzzlement of an ape contemplating its own reflection and then remembered. His own flushed, bloodshot reflection duly swam into focus and he turned away.

There being no one for Tom to disturb he spoke aloud slowly, with an anger and sincerity that moved even himself.

'You get modern. You get so-phis-ti-cated. You read up. You inquire. About people, about yourself, society. About the truth behind blah blah blah… And you discover, well, fuck me sideways, lies are not just part of the fabric here – they're essential to it. So how do we cope? Yup, we get ironic. 'Hey! Watch me live so knowingly, so smart and detached, so brand-aware and sterile, so self-ab-fucking-sorbed … and you know what's even cooler? I don't believe in one fucking ounce of my own life. Not one. Cos – hadn't you heard? – believing in anything beyond your own needs is just too naïve, darling, just too quaint and so excruciatingly twentieth century.' Well, you know what I want to know? All I want to know is what comes after irony? Because it's not going to be enough.'

'Fourteen fifty will do me the now, pal!' a voice crackled in his ear.

He'd discovered enough notes stuffed into his trouser pockets from bar change to cover the taxi fare. The entry system for the tenement had never worked. His own door was too solid to run at. The hinges were recessed. The Yale lock might as well have been superglued. There was no way he could scale three floors and enter by the window nor had he ever got round to stashing spare keys anywhere. Neighbours? His policy towards them reflected theirs towards him – polite avoidance – so he couldn't think seriously about disturbing them this late. There was no one close enough to call either. Besides, his phone was with his keys and wallet in his bag under the table at Black Bo's.

He would have to crash here tonight and then tomorrow he would get his bag from the bar. He crumpled onto a cold stone step in the bend of the stair, yanked his jacket tight round him and turned up his collar. After a few minutes he dragged the doormat over to lie on.

With his wallet and ID gone he couldn't prove who he was. Not that he would need to really, but the idea was disconcerting. It was alarming how dependent his identity was on objects, and how easily they could be lost. He wondered about the dormant sense of security – no, belonging – that he took for granted each day. Because as far as tonight was concerned, he was no longer part of the tenement, the neighbourhood, the city or of anything at all.

He was restless now. Maybe a little panicked. He opened his eyes, peered up to the floors above and down to those below. It was no doubt for reasons akin to contagion that most of the residents had those weak night-lights in their halls. The glow from them passed through the oblong windows above their doors subtly decorating the stairwell. Here and there a stained-glass splash of vivid, translucent blues, yellows, greens and reds stretched across the glossy grey council paint. But the more they caught his eye, the more Tom grew resentful. In there, having wound down their day, people were comfortable. They would be yawning, stretching and curling up with someone warm until they slid down, millimetre by gentle millimetre, into a deep, serene sleep.

He struggled upright and leaned heavily against his own door. It felt warm against his cheek and his eyes closed. He placed a palm on one of the grainy panels as though trying to think it open, but all he could imagine were the hinges tensing deep within the door's spine and the lock digging in. Memories from the other side flowed but oddly not the big ticket possessions: the telescope, computer or sound system. First it was his birth certificate and passport. Next his fingerprints on taps and his sofa with his contours. Then the weird clouds of his hair, shed skin and dust that gathered in corners. Then it was the peculiarities he remembered. Things that he had tinkered with or made work. Things that bore his mark. And finally, it was something so absolutely familiar to Tom as to be detectable only by others. The smell as you opened the door.

A toilet flushing somewhere. So many sounds were lost during the day but at night the building's angled planes of steel, stone, concrete, glass, wood and plaster became transmitters, amplifiers. Perhaps there would be solace in a sort of proxy domesticity. Creeping to the banister Tom stood with head cocked, listening closely. Taps running. Silence. Footsteps. A fridge door closing with a dampened whump and rattle. A dog yelping somewhere, hushed by its owner. Nothing. Then, along to his left, a kettle boiling and cutlery clashing in a drawer. A couple arguing in strained murmurs, pauses and sudden crescendos. The high gurgling and gibberish of an infant.

Sleep was impossible now. He had to get out so he shuffled downstairs past other people's lives.

It was good to be moving. Purpose felt good. Arriving at the park he creaked open the ancient gate and found his favourite bench. It was set back from the main path crossing the park and just beyond the pools of yellow from the streetlights that lined it like sentinels. Squinting across the path he could dimly make out three familiar trees. The central one, a stolid, impressive oak with leaves that stretched out in every direction, was flanked by two striplings. Like nature's Christ crucified and the two thieves. What were the names of those two again?

Beyond, and fainter still, the local church spire pierced the night sky. This arrangement of shapes – the bench, the grass, trees and church – Tom found inexplicably soothing. This was a benign place. Tonight, though, with his body, his head, his solitary future, everything feeling so tired and heavy, his mind wouldn't settle. He studied the trees. Was this it? The truth behind all truths? Something was creeping up on him. In his bones it felt like he'd had enough pointless, vain cognition for one lifetime. Enough agency without a purpose and enough gutting uncertainty. He let out a deep sigh. Something in his chest cried out for release, longed to surrender. It felt as though he'd been hunted down and finally run to ground by religion, by God himself. But this wasn't supposed to happen. Everything was sliding from him. What comes after irony? This. *Suffer little children*, he remembered from childhood, *and forbid them not to come unto me*. I'll be a kid again, he thought flatly: I'll be as a child before God.

Then, as though a street play had commenced solely for his benefit, two figures appeared from nowhere, jogging along the path. Were it not for the pushchair they would have been running. They each wore an immaculate white baseball cap and sunglasses. As they passed beneath successive cones of yellow light, they seemed to gently pulse. He watched their approach as though hypnotised and with an anticipation in his belly that made him feel slightly sick.

The man, in baggy tracksuit bottoms and a polo shirt, strode ahead talking into his mobile phone with his free hand down his underpants. The woman, a large blemish on her neck, kept up with him while shoving the pushchair. From her other hand jutted a cigarette. The child was swaddled in a pale blanket. Tom craned his neck to get a better view of it. It too pulsed, bright gold then fading to amber. But the shape of it was not right at all. Unnatural. The pushchair cradled not a child at all but a matt, black plastic box. A games console. The man noticed him sitting on the bench. He stopped, looked over at Tom but kept the phone to his ear,

'Awright? Fuck ye up tae? … Hi! You! Ye deaf?'

'…Oh, me? Sorry. Yeah, I'm alright.' Strangely disappointed, Tom added vaguely, 'Just… waiting.'

'Aye, ye are in't ye… Wasted, aye? Ye holdin'?'

'No. Just sitting here. Got nothing. Nothing at all.'

The man jerked his head away and barked into the phone. 'Nah, no you ya fuckin' mong! Goat a sorty poash cunt here, like. Says he's got nowt, but… aye… aye. Hud oan then.' He turned back to Tom. 'Hi, you! Y'after any'hin' then?'

'No. Not really.' He desperately needed to go to the toilet.

Sizing him up the man continued into the phone, 'Nah… says he's no' interested, like. Naw, forget it, man. Hud oan. Hud oan.' His body, until now busy with tics and gestures, grew still, as though something had occurred to him. 'Eh… phone eez later.'

Dropping the phone into his back pocket the man appeared to scrutinise the dark sky through his sunglasses for a moment. He scratched his baseball cap then moved in. He leaned slowly down and brought a broad smile and rotten teeth in close to Tom's face. The woman by the pushchair lifted her gaze away sharply to the horizon. Tom saw the blemish was a dragon tattoo. She slackened a hip, placed a forearm across her swollen belly and on it rested her other elbow as she sucked hard on the cigarette. Smoke billowed around her head gracefully as the smouldering tip flared.

'For fucksake get a move on, G!' she said.

'Awright awright. Now. You. Posh cunt. Vic. You need an Xbox an' that's that. Fuckin works an' aw. Ah'd swear on ma unborn's.'

Tom's eyes flicked nervously to the console then off to one side, trying not to bite through his cheek.

'S'matter? Naw, naw, naw nae worries. Ah'm no' like that. Ah widnae take the blade ooty ma back poakit and use it oan ye. Widnae blind ye just like that!' His flattened hand sliced past Tom's temple. 'Now do Ah look the kindae gadge who'd dae that, eh? No way, man!' G had a foot on the bench now, one hand on Tom's shoulder and a finger pointing in his face. He whispered, 'Less Ah hud tae, like. Ken whit Ah'm sayin?' He leaned back, 'So… yours for fifty quid, right?'

'I've nothing on me.' His mouth had dried up and he was trembling, but he managed to meet G's eyes.

'Aye right! Says he's nuthin' oan him, Dee. Ye believe that? Yev nuthin' oan ye?' Gee pulled his hands back, curled them into two fists and put a menacing snarl on his face. Through clenched teeth came, 'Nuthin', is it Vic?'

Tom had no energy to shield himself, nor the will to. Nor could he hold G's eyes any longer. Whatever strength had been left in him had dissolved but something raised him to his feet and shaped his hands into loose, unaccustomed fists. Amazed, he threw one out pathetically but instantly found himself sitting back on the bench with a stinging eye. His head dropped to see blood splashing to his feet from his nose. How had that happened? There was a strange, timeless lull – Tom thought he heard the muted clang of the church bell – before a backhand cracked into his cheekbone. Sprawled along the bench now, stunned, he was unaware of the large dark stain forming at his crotch. Just the faint warmth.

Dee rolled her eyes. 'Aw for fucksake look at that! Let's go. Leave him. Danny'll hae fucked oaf!'

'Awright! Nip, nip, nip! Christ, man.' G shook out his hands and patted down Tom's empty jacket. 'Aw ferfuksake!' He unleashed a flurry of kicks to Tom's shin then turned to go, but stopped. 'Yer shoes. Now that Ahv wiped ma arse wi ye Ahm havin' yer fuckin shoes.' Tom could only lie there slack and dazed. 'OK, Victim?'

He felt tugging and twisting and stamping at his feet until both shoes were gone. G skipped, laughed wildly and leaped away with the two trophies held high in the air.

'Ah, ya fuckin' mug! Ha, haha! You better toughin up, son. It's a fuckin' jungle oot here!'

Birdsong echoed round the park and the sun blazed, not yet clearing the city skyline. When its rays reached Tom's hand the hairs rose in tingling gooseflesh. One eye fluttered open; the other was tight shut. His cheek, pounding dully a few feet away, glided back in to where it belonged. A fine dew had settled over everything while he slept. Diamonds of it fell sideways from the leaf-tips of the oak tree onto a smashed wine bottle with a steady tap, tap, tap. It covered crisp bags and grass shoots and crept down the chains that held plastic swing seats where the children played.

Tom levered himself upright and tried to stand. The stabbing pain from his legs was nasty but nothing was broken. The small stones jabbing into his stockinged feet weren't as sore but he'd never make it all the way to Black Bo's. That didn't seem to matter. Things couldn't get any worse. Something simple, clear and hard formed and it filled him with a perverse exaltation. He walked over to the damp grass and removed his socks for the hell of it.

'Within every instant lies every possible future!' he announced to the empty park. That might even be true, he thought. The Yale knob had to be rotated. Pulleys turn knobs. That was all. This was only going to be as complicated as it needed to be.

It only took him fifteen minutes to gather from the gutters and skips and bins of the neighbourhood the materials he needed. Two lengths of string, and to tie between them one short length of thin, plastic-coated electrical wire with, luckily, just the right slightly sticky feel. The thumbnail-sized lump of roofing lead he'd tie to one end of string and an old coat hanger would serve as a grabbing hook. It was just a question of time before he got the release trajectory correct. He was a monkey, after all. And this was infinity.

A JUDGE OF CHARACTER
by Johnny Acton

'Cally please.'

Three short plump white people squeezed themselves into the car. Typical Sunday lunchtime fodder.

'Do you reckon you're a good judge of character?' asked the father, a little balding guy with a bit of a twinkle. Old school cockney, no 'bruvs' or 'innits'. Touch of the Victorian about him.

'Not bad.' I said, noncommittally.

'Fancy taking part in an experiment?' he asked.

I could feel his wife squirm slightly in the seat behind me. Evidently she was not unfamiliar with this routine. The son, who I'd put at about twelve, was organically coupled with his mobile.

'Go on then,' I said.

'How much is this fare? About a tenner?'

'Something like that.'

'Ok then, let's play minicab roulette. I'm going to stick a note under my shoe. It might be a fiver or it might be a score. When you drop us off, I'll pay you the ten if you like, or you can take a punt on what kind of person I am and go for what's under my foot. It's up to you entirely. Am I a mean bastard or a philanthropist?' He lay back in his seat, placing his arms behind his head and revealing himself to be no devotee of Right Guard. If he didn't actually start whistling, he might as well have done.

As we swerved along the greasy, windswept back streets that I could and often did negotiate in my sleep, I mused upon the likely meaning of this performance. Was the whole thing a cautionary tale for his boy, an illustration from the manual of the academy of hard knocks? 'You see son? Life's a bitch. Never trust anyone. They'll only let you down.' Was it the opposite – a demonstration of largesse, proof positive that he was a mensch? Or was it just a mild way of torturing his other half?

I looked in the mirror at the wife's cross/amused expression and the spectacular lack of interest from the son. These people didn't seem particularly put upon.

As we pulled up, I announced my decision. 'Right, well all things considered, I'm going for the note under the shoe.' Dad lifted his foot in theatrical slow motion, revealing... a twenty. 'Good for you mate!' he pronounced, unfolding the note and handing it to me with a flourish. He seemed genuinely pleased. 'May I ask why you called it like you did?'

'Sure,' I said. 'I took you this way about six months ago.'

He couldn't have been more delighted.

Pyramid
by JP Fitch

'It's just a game…' Lano repeats it like a mantra, over and over, ad finitum. He's looking at me with his maniac smile, thin lips parted like razor sliced flesh exposing his yellowing gravestone teeth.

'It's all just a fucking game… know what I mean, Little Man?'

I nod.

'We were all just little pieces of plastic to them, and they pushed us around, moving us into place. We didn't have a choice before. We didn't have a fucking chance. That's what Malky says, anyway. Ask him, he'll tell you, he'll fucking tell you alright.'

Lano chuckles. The assembly hall stinks of petrol. All of the desks and chairs from the classrooms are piled up into a pyramid in the middle of the hall. He opens the last can of petrol and begins to splash it around. Tattered paper decorations of the solar system hang from the dark ceiling, the heavenly bodies dotted around in haphazard fashion with the sun as the centerpiece, directly above the apex of the structure we've built.

A winged thing buzzes close by in the gloom. I swat at the darkness but it's already gone, hunting, or being hunted. The air feels alive in here: it teems and ticks with the clacking tiny wings of a million insects harboured in the mass of vegetation that climbs the inner walls of the decrepit school. The vines and creepers reach to the ceiling like leafy veins. I feel like I'm inside a living skeleton, dead yet not dead at the same time.

'When this is done, can we get some chips?'

Lano stops. 'Chip shop's been closed down for years, Little Man. Remember?'

'Yeah… just thought… y'know…'

He hollers and grabs me in a headlock, squeezing tight, his biceps bulging into the back of my neck. It feels like all my blood is trapped in my skull and the pressure is building, but I force a laugh. 'C'mon,' he says, letting go and running a thick hand over his shaved head, 'let's get finished and join the others. I hear they caught a Plodder. Should be good tonight. Bonfire Night is always great.'

Everyone is waiting for us in the library; Jamesy, Billy-boy, Pirate, Twigs, Dit-dot, The Feral Twins; everyone except Big Bruvs and Malky. Lano swaggers into their midst. He's easily the biggest of us all, outwith Malky.

'Where the fuck have you two been?' says Pirate, 'We're all waiting on you two cunts.'

'Calm yer jets. We're here now. Where's Malky then?' Lano says.

'Dunno. Big Bruvs is bringing up the Plodder instead.'

'Where'd ya find him?' I say.

Pirate spins and smacks me on the cheek with the back of his hand. I feel it burn. Even though he's smaller than me, he's as mean as a rabid dog. Pirate has been in more fights and taken more beatings from the Plodders than any of us. One night three of them caught him after he set fire to the old Plodder shop down by the gasworks. They'd taken one of his eyes that night and left him for dead.

'Shut it, cunt,' says Pirate, 'You don't get to fuckin' talk. Anyway, found him hiding in the chapel up the road. He'd been there for weeks, empty tins of soup and spaghetti lying all about the place. He'd been shitting in a bag so he didn't have to go outside. Crafty cunt.'

We nod in silent agreement. My stomach tightens.

The double doors are kicked open and in staggers the Plodder. He sprawls on the ground, broken and smashed. Malky has taken liberties with him as he always does with the old 'uns he catches. The Plodder's nose is shattered and he's missing an ear (Malky's souvenir), but for some reason the worst thing is the dress that he's been made to wear. It's white and puffy and seems several sizes too small for him, but he's been squeezed into it. Gone is the uniform. Malky has probably burned it – that's what he does with everything. The boys are all laughing but I can't laugh, so I wear a plastic smile while I wince inside. They haven't beaten the last of my compassion out of me, not yet. I still keep a sliver of the old me in there. It's something to hold on to during the bad times.

It's shameful what Malky's done to the Plodder and he knows it. His once arrogant eyes are puffy and bruised, and underneath the swollen flesh I see only fear. I catch his eye for an instant expecting a vengeful gaze but see only deep pools of shame. Malky has broken his spirit. He is no longer a man. Perhaps he never was? Perhaps he hid behind that uniform the whole time, pretending?

He staggers and trips. A cry goes up and the boys pounce on him like animals, whooping and hollering and reeling; the monkey dance has begun. Amid the chaos a wooden club is brought down on the back of the Plodders neck. It makes a sickening crack and he tumbles from the blow. The boys haul him up by his hair, by his armpits, by his remaining ear; fingers hooking the delicate flesh of his cheek and pulling, tearing. The Plodder cries out and Billy-boy punches him in the face twice, three times. The Plodder sags like he's made of straw. Thick blood runs from his mouth like a crimson river with teeth like small boats caught in the wash.

The gang hoist the plodder and carry him through to the adjacent hall to the petrol soaked pyramid that Lano and I built earlier. My stomach knots and I feel sick. This is the part I hate; the screaming and the thrashing, and the laughing of the boys.

The smell of petrol pinches my nose. The boys work quickly, hauling the plodder up onto the pyramid. The desks creak and moan with the weight and the movement. Soon he lies prostrate on its peak, a meat capstone. Lano hands me a box. The boys go silent and stare at me.

I look at the matches and my stomach lurches again.

'It's what Malky wants,' he says, quietly.

I look up at Lano with wet eyes and he nods balefully. 'Go on Little Man,' he says, 'It's just a fuckin' game.'

The match sparks on the third stroke. The flame dances and flickers. In the silence, the Plodder wakes and begins to moan in pain.

I drop the match.

The flames take the pyramid quickly, working up towards the Plodder, like wolves after a lame deer. The dress catches and goes up and begins to melt onto the Plodders skin, and the boys begin to dance and sing and scream and howl and the Plodder cries and shrieks with lungs of fire and I feel every burning breath he takes.

I begin to cry. Lano puts his arm around my shoulders and I turn into him, burying my face in his chest and covering my ears. I yell to block out the sound of the Plodder and the chanting of the boys and the smell of roasting meat. After the longest time the Plodder goes quiet and lies still and the fire consumes him.

We stand outside as the sun rises. Lano pats me on the back as I finish retching onto the grass. The other boys mill around throwing stones at the windows of the school as the fire consumes it with growing hatred. The school is a crumbling wall, standing defiantly against the red sky. It won't be long till it's gone completely. Nature will take care of that, like it does with everything.

'Don't worry Little Man. It gets better. The first one is always the hardest. I remember when Malky caught old Mr Hughes, the geography teacher, back when it was dangerous, when the Plodders were still fighting back. Malky scalped old Hughesy… took a bread knife and hacked the top of his head right off, sickest thing I ever seen.'

I look at Lano; he's staring off into the distance with a pained look on his face. He turns to me and smiles sadly. 'I liked old Hughes. He wasn't a bad 'un. He didn't deserve that.'

He gets up and begins walking towards the boys. 'Come on. Malky's waiting for us down by the Chapel. Maybe he's found another Plodder? They always hang about in twos or threes.'

The Birthday Surprise
by Marcelle Thiébaux

When Daisy Rilsko turned fourteen on St. Valentine's Day, 1932, her grandmother barged into her bedroom with a birthday surprise. She set a saucer with a slice of pink-frosted cake on the foot of Daisy's bed.

'Birthday surprise!' Madame Zynovia sang out cheerful as a breeze. 'And I don't want any back talk.' Svelte in her black Duchess of Windsor daytime dress, she kicked the door shut behind her and leaned against it. Folded her arms. 'You have a nice new life ahead of you.'

Daisy stopped brushing. Aureole of sunshiny daffodil hair. Bare baby-goddess tits, ninety-nine pounds in sugar white panties, she sat down all at once at her vanity table. She cut a sullen glare at the fat slab of cake on her bed, the pink frosting studded with blood red cinnamon dot-hearts. Two old pink candles sagging.

'Now what?' she demanded.

'A lovely time. Clothes, jewellery, gentlemen. Lots of them. We bring the gentlemen right here to our own house on the boulevard. We'll show you what to do and how to do it.'

Madame Zynovia talked faster, a little out of breath about the birthday surprise. 'You'll meet the richest gents. Mayors, moguls, magistrates. Home-loving heads of families, even college boys. And don't give me school. You had too much school. It made you stupid. You're getting ideas. And eyeglasses are simply out of the question. Don't interrupt me. What man wants a girl with her nose in a book? Look at me. You have to admit how good I look.'

Madame Zynovia posed, hand on hip. Her carmine lips quivered in an effort to smile naturally so she lit up a Lucky Strike. Drew in. Blew out a curl of hot smoke.

Daisy's thin little fingers rested in her vanity drawer and closed around the .25 revolver. Her grandmother thought it was still nailed shut in the box she'd hid in the kitchen. Daisy had found the box days ago behind the flour sifter. Pried it open with a chisel. Snuck the gun into her room.

Today was the third anniversary of the Valentine's Day massacre. Those Chicago guys with machine guns. They mowed down a bunch of gangsters in a beer warehouse, blood all over the cement floor. Bodies. Daisy remembered the newspapers. The grainy photos. But Daisy was a girl. A girl would get away with it for sure.

Walking Bibi
by David Cameron

Bibi has what I need. I walk him all hours in this druggy park. We go round the lake and he sniffs the ducks – they have no fear here. Nobody has any fear.

I send him into the bushes and he brings back the stick and I send him in again, and then the men come out, the young one first, the hustler, who if he recognises me always laughs. Bibi knows these boys too. I'd pass the time of day with them, but they have nothing to say. Little at first and, later, nothing.

I like the entrance. Next to it is a hotel called Shalimar. If I could afford another animal, I'd call it that. Bibi's too old to be renamed, and I like the name Bibi now. Mother gave him it. She's psychic, everybody knows, yet she can't tell the sex of an animal. Can't pay that much attention.

I think I've exhausted this park, then something new turns up. I find out a girl was discovered in leaf mould the year I was born. It was near the hyacinths. There was a service. Hyacinths were planted. If there was a plaque on some tree or bench, it's been ripped out. That was the right thing to do: parks are for the living. I'm not going to confuse the bitches that surround Bibi by putting him in the ground here when he goes.

Bin day tomorrow, so there's that to look forward to. Here nothing good's put out, nothing to sell on I mean, though it's all right for a clothes horse for instance. I saw a man on the street yesterday pushing the buttons of a hi-fi. He wasn't too badly dressed either. Reminded me of a refugee I spoke to on a balcony at a party once. Had an iron cross on his chest. Smelled awful, but so what? So did I. Except he had a proper place. He spoke a lot about his place, how near and how nice it was. I blanked him. It only made him more interested.

No, I know where to go on nights before bin days. Not the streets tourists flock to before the weather turns. One street in particular I like: New Mirror Street. There are some poor there – they have a deal going that means they never leave. Only the rich sometimes move out, and what they don't want I take. I'm not the only one, God knows. But if stuff's in my hands, sweetheart, try taking it from me. (I talk like this sometimes. Don't be put off. When I bark, Bibi barks, and that soothes me. Then I can hold my breath for five minutes at a time.)

I met my ex in this park. I saw all this as a kid, was wheeled through the gates out of the park, looked up at the same old clock on the burnt church. Now it's mainly offices. I don't mind, I hated that gloomy church. Though old people could doze in it when the park was freezing. The gates are the same too. Wonderful wrought iron, with a design you think is dragons but is only plant stems. Now the man who made those gates, I'd like to speak to him for a day. Just listen and nod sometimes and let him ask me about Bibi and anything he wanted really. I wouldn't mind sitting beside a man like that.

I'm not in the mood for the market today. All that fowl hanging upside down and making Bibi excited. I'd sooner take my chances in the museum. When you're hungry you can cope with the smell of must better than the smell of roasting chicken. It's my own fault. I shouldn't walk so much. Walking is always fatal. Each day I tell myself I'll stay still tomorrow. Tomorrow comes and I'm halfway round the city before I remember. Why should I complain? Bibi doesn't. I see hunger in his eyes sometimes, and I love him so much for trying to hide it.

'Cappuccino, with nutmeg,' I tell the boy in the coffee cart. Whenever I feel poor, I spend money. This won't be much, and I avoid looking down at Bibi. There's nothing for you here, boy, anyway.

I'm talking to my dog.

I am called Femke. Some think it a beautiful name, others not. I've no opinion. That's who I am and I have to live with it. I'm not suggesting anyone call their daughter Femke. I think it's older people who like it best. Maybe there were more Femkes in their day. I'd say Femke was Mother's choice, because of the two syllables, like Bibi. I have a sister called Annemieke and that was Father's doing. He'd tease mother that this was the name of the sweetheart who left him so devastated he was like an empty room for Mother to walk into. By the way Mother smiled I knew it was true. Father's dead now.

I am prettier than Annemieke. Nevertheless, she was always, and still is, everyone's favourite. (I exclude boys from this 'everyone'.) I've had a habit since I was twelve of tilting back my head and rolling my eyes till the whites show. Tests revealed I 'elect to do it', which makes me hateful. I don't have visions or say anything memorable, though I do moan – 'eerily', I am told.

There's a Chinese proverb: cut a blade of grass and you shake the universe. When I heard that, from the ex I met in the park (it was our first meeting), I tore handfuls and handfuls of grass in a frenzy. That's not how I changed the world though. Nobody believes this. I was in a gallery – I'd gone because there was an opening where there'd be free wine. It was a nothing show, and I said this to the homosexual beside me. He looked me up and down in a way I know all too well. Then I got it: he was eyeing up my clothes. Those days – like everyone now – I wore baggy trousers that scraped the ground. The homosexual was puzzled and then thoughtful. He asked if I couldn't find something more my size. I said 'What if I elect not to?' and his eyes lit up. I know the things to say to make men's eyes do that, but clearly I wasn't trying now. He asked all sorts of questions. By the time he gave me his business card and said he was a famous fashion designer and could he look me up, I was bored senseless. I gave him *my* business card then. Well, I resented spilling myself out like that for a queer.

It's nothing but a big barn where I live. There'll be people there when it's offices. The work keeps getting put back. I've lived in a place like it before, also near the harbour. I'd sneak old friends in and out till everyone got too casual and I couldn't shift them even on days when the owner came round. I don't make the same mistake twice. It's not as if I have to explain myself. My name was mud in the squats long ago.

This place has no running water, just a chemical toilet the owner sees to. He comes round: I almost look forward to it. He's got a bronzed complexion – maybe has a timeshare in a hot climate – and a man-in-his-mid-40s' paunch. Still thinks he can run it off.

He made a move on me once while showing me the gas heater. It came as a surprise. I hadn't been shown how to use one before and was quite interested – if I could be anything I'd be an electrician or engineer. We were both hunkered, but his knees had cracked a second or so before he put a hand on my knee. 'I think not,' was what I said. (Quite proud of that 'I think not'.) He said it had just been to balance himself. I didn't laugh. Now he mews around the place for half an hour then leaves.

There are advantages to being pretty. You know that the men who are nasty to you are psychopaths. Today you'd do well to make out my looks – I could care if there was a point. I don't want to be drawing too many glances in these streets. Men can be cruel, but when I look hard at them and they see me better, they change their tune. Except the psychos. Bibi is handy for them. He's part Alsatian. I wouldn't say he spots them a mile off, but he knows when I'm distressed.

I did get entangled with one psycho. I blame the virus that laid me low at the time. It hurts me to say it, but he looked a lot like Van Gogh. I have an affection for that bearded misfit and not just because I'm fond of foxgloves and fields of wheat. The psycho was in tweeds even though he was practically homeless. He was all right except when I flirted with him. You have to flirt to make the days less dull. I spent a month in his company.

He had a passion for identifying bodies. Told the police his sister was missing and could he check any stiffs they had. I laughed at all this because it's funny. Less funny when the man is next to you drooling over the word 'suppurating'. We would walk along and look into houses, and he would really fume at all the softness we saw. Well I've felt that way too, but I was nostalgic for it at the same time. I told him so. He threw me down and tried to break my head on a bollard.

I wish I felt the cold less. I would seriously like my puppy fat back. Annemieke probably still has hers. In her case, it might never be lost. She lives with Mother in a sort of suburban existence that's the same the world over. So I imagine. Even when we all lived in the city we had a summerhouse. It was in one of those depressing beehives of summerhouses on the outskirts, where nobody gets buried in leaf mould, and the dragonflies are the size of your hand. I found it impossible to feel haunted there. Couldn't even throw my head back.

Father died on my twelfth birthday.

There's this one place I eat where the waitress exposes an inch or two of her middle and it's just a seam of fat. She's not bad-looking, she just has that seam of fat. I'd love to roll it between my fingers. People can't tell with my jumper and parka how thin I can be. Because it does vary. Six months ago if I'd spun like a coin, I'd've vanished.

Mother often had premonitions she'd speak about afterwards. I can't square the mother I knew as a kid with the suburban Mama of now. Back then she was a witch. Father, I think, thought so – I could see he was in awe of her. She used to brew a weird concoction to keep from catching a cold. She was something of a singer in those days. Strictly small-time operettas. I got a tongue-lashing once when I tried her cold medicine, though the taste was punishment enough. It makes me think now that it had a strong lacing of alcohol. She was capable of drinking during the day. Once Father was gone, I had visions of us losing everything. Mother becoming a Baby Jane. Or perhaps that has happened, and she spends her days tormenting Annemieke, with rat for supper. A girl can dream.

My weirdness I blamed on her. This was in the time of tests. I remember sills and sills of spider plants in a long corridor with mad paintings along it. The first time Mother really hit me was to get me out of a trance. Then it became punishment for going into one.

Her job was to have old friends round and do their hair for them. I expect there was too much time spent alone, alone or with us. The way she stared through us, it was almost the same thing. (No, something in Annemieke held her attention.) At least we had dead hair to play with.

I'd watch Mother fill up with emptiness between phone-calls, in the hours waiting for Father to come. I liked those mornings when she was on the phone and sounding animated, I didn't care how much, I never feared her manic side. I knew we were in for a good day then. What scared me was her monotone. (I shivered just then, thinking about it, and I was already shivering.)

She was suspicious of me. I fed her suspicions without wanting to. The only time I took a man home and we fucked in her double bed, she knew. She got back from a weekend away and shook me to find out what I'd done. As she was shaking me, I saw a pair of my socks under her bed. She hadn't seen those, or they would have been all the proof she needed. *Christ, you are a witch*, I thought. *You made me leave them there*. I got them back when she was out the room. They had thin blue and black stripes. I've never worn socks with stripes since.

She had suspected Father too. There were odd words, tears, famously a plate smeared with ketchup thrown against a wall (blood, I told my friends), which I understood suddenly: Father was having an affair. I doubt this now. He did have a glamorous secretary, possibly a succession of them, I only ever saw the one.

My sole time in Daddy's office. There was a man called Clark or Clerk – Clark Kent was a name I knew – who stood the whole time Father sat. I remember Father's voice being softer than in the house. Africa was mentioned. I'd been given a toy snake with brown and beige scales and was playing with it. The secretary appeared as she was about to leave. She was wearing white gloves.

Talking about Father's death won't warm me up. One thing, though: it made us richer. Now that the money's gone – or more likely tied up in something – I'm glad. It's cleaner that way.

I learned all about men once Father was dead. A beautiful widow and two pubescent girls are not nothing. They came sniffing round, pawed us a little, ran off, then they'd come sniffing back. (Why do I lie? We were safe enough in our house. Only the insurance man – Mother had a lot of dealings with him – got further than the doorstep.) Mother's body had thickened before grief went to work on it. In the photo I have of the three of us from then, taken by some monkey making a display before Mother, she is alarmingly beautiful.

Holidays were worst. One man I remember: I called him Shoe Shuffle Man. We had just stepped off the boat when mechanically the music started up – twenty minutes it played for – and Mother did three or four steps of a dance with Annemieke. Always the same steps, danced from girlhood on, maybe to this day. Shoe Shuffle Man appeared, sliding his moccasins across the planks, arms raised in a 'May I?' gesture, but of course directed towards Annemieke in order to get to Mother, who was now walking smartly into the reception area. A smoker's laugh and a few words of song, which Mother foolishly turned and smiled back at. He dogged us the whole holiday then. There was only the promenade, so it was easy for him. His grey-blue trousers – slacks, he'd have said – were perfectly pressed. Why does that generation of men hate women? Mother despised them. She felt she shouldn't, but she did. Father at least had something gutsy about him, looked almost like Robert Mitchum at times. He must have seemed an odd fish to those slacked shufflers. Those Clarks or Clerks.

Innocence Lost
by Charles E McGarry

Elaine used to live with the cosy assumption that up until her sister Jennifer's disappearance hers had been a dull, relatively cosseted childhood, ensconced as it was within their brown suburb, safely removed from the mean streets of the tough old city. Until one day while she was idly reminiscing she realised that it had, in fact, been an era peppered with several startling incursions from the badlands beyond the elms.

She pictured her child self, the peripheral participant, that quiet, serious, watchful little girl. Eyes screwed into slits and freckled cheeks pinched against the light as she gazed downwards from the suntrap of their patio at the activity in the back lane below.

The first memory that occurred to her, the most disturbing and the one that triggered her remembrance of the rest, was that of the Stranger. She recalled, blurrily, a real-life car chase just like the ones her dad liked watching on *Kojak* and *The Sweeney*. A red Mk1 Ford Escort, sunlight sparkling on the chrome, being driven at speed down the lane which was teeming with children, pursued by a squad car (a quaintly incongruous sky-blue and white VW Beetle), emergency light spinning and two-tone siren blaring, Jennifer and the other older girls whisking the younger kids into garage inlets in the nick of time (so Elaine remembered it anyway).

Then there was the day of the mad dog, a salivating mongrel, its black-and-gold coat somehow rendered more vital in the fierce sunshine as it scattered hysterical children. Mr Greaves, an Anzio veteran, fearlessly scooping toddlers into his strong arms as he fended off the beast with his right Hush Puppy. A grey Commer van with the Glasgow Corporation logo on the side arriving to take the creature away and destroy it. There was the day when Mr McGregor's Datsun Cherry spontaneously burst into flames; the fierce, rushing heat, acrid poison spewing into the air, a mushroom of steam and smoke when the Fire Brigade doused the inferno. There was the burglar who had established himself in Mr Woods' cellar during daylight, and – horror movie style – patiently waited until the early hours when he crept through the hatch only to be discovered by the householder who had come downstairs to fetch a glass of water. Mr Woods (known locally as simply 'The Bachelor') yelling profanities as he gave chase along the lane in his funny little underpants. There was the incident of the unexploded German bomb, police vehicles crawling the roads and drives, warning residents through loudhailers to stay indoors and keep away from the windows, a chilling rehearsal for the four-minute warning everybody dreaded. And – the vaguest of memories this one; probably the details filled in by her mother years later – that terrible January night when Mr Anderson and his two boys emerged through the freezing fog like ghosts, Mrs Anderson kneeling like a prophet on the cold pavement as she wept, her relief coming out as anger, her husband gently explaining that they couldn't get use of a telephone to reassure her, that they had been on the periphery of the crush – the tragic scale of which they simply had not imagined – and had needed to take a little time to recover themselves. Then they had had to walk all the way home from Ibrox stadium because by then the police had closed off the road which led to the Subway station.

But the episode of the Stranger had cast the deepest shadow over the long, hot summer that it invaded. What was actually done to Micky Gallacher behind old Mrs Mackay's derelict garage Elaine would never know. She would only recall that in the aftermath, which was a maelstrom of rage and confusion, the boy's face was puffy and chafed crimson from weeping. She had looked on guiltily as her mother impotently implored her father, Mr Greaves, Mr Woods and Mr Anderson for restraint while Mrs Greaves and Mrs Anderson rushed to telephone the proper authorities. Guiltily because the Stranger had initially seemed harmless if rather malodorous, and she and Wee Karen had tolerated his company and unwittingly encouraged him as they naively continued with their task of making a jam jar of perfume from crushed rose petals. But from their tender perspective the man had seemed too young, too good-looking to fit the bill of the predators their minds had been terrorised with at school.

Some time later the men returned in miserable silence, and Elaine, who had been sitting in the living room when her father stomped in, had been too frightened and shocked to move, and so endured the heavy quiet that dragged out between them, punctuated only by the idiotic ticking of the mantle clock as her dad gazed angrily into a fixed point in space, offended by something impenetrably grown-up and unspeakably gross, his face grey, his raw knuckles trembling slightly as they gripped the arms of the Parker Knoll. The shock of her father, her *daddy*, fastened down by some primal violence, snapping at her mother when she tried to bathe his hand; her gentle father who had spanked her brother only occasionally and only half-heartedly and only when he had been really bad. It would emerge via adult conversations earwigged from the top stair that the men had cornered the interloper down by the Nature Walk, under the road bridge which spanned the railway. Those being different days, the duty-bound CID man who wearily rang the doorbell seemed readily assuaged by Elaine's father's laconic denials and his quite reasonable observation that the fellow had got off lightly. Had Micky's father, Big Jack, not been away from home that day attending to business, he would undoubtedly have committed murder. As it happens the deviant would not see that year out, dying in a jailhouse brawl as he waited for a trial date on an unrelated matter. Anyway, later that day Elaine's father loosened up and, obviously feeling guilty at the effect his earlier mood must have had on his family, he called Elaine to him. She obeyed, but received his sentimental embrace reluctantly, her body as stiff as a board, her senses repelled by the smell of Scotch and cigarette smoke, her face still rigid with a vague fear.

This same energy, awful yet righteous, that had driven her father to commit such mischief, revealed itself again after Jennifer's disappearance three years later, but it had ebbed quite rapidly as he descended into a vortex of anxiety and sorrow. It was as though the very life force had drained from him. He wept more openly than his wife, who maintained a stoical, dignified manner. Yet like her husband Mrs Bowman would implode through ill health. Both would die prematurely, a fact no one doubted was caused by loss of their daughter. As for Elaine, her initial shock and denial were tinged with a strange type of envy of people for the continued, unruffled banality of their lives. And as the surreal unreality of the catastrophe abated, these feelings gave way to agonising grief, which in turn transmuted into a slow, deadly anger as the dividing line between Everything That Happened Before and Everything That Happened After settled like the tissue of a vicious scar.

However, the loving upbringing she had enjoyed could sustain her during the bleak years ahead, and she would not allow this rage to consume her as it had her father. She would wield it with the awesomeness with which he had confronted the pervert in the Nature Walk that day, but she would retain control of it. It would be laser-focused; it would become her driving force – even if she had to wait a lifetime.

Now, thirty years on, the faceless beast who had stolen Elaine's sister away had finally broken cover and struck again: same location, same victim profile, same MO. And this time he had left clues – definite leads which years of honing her skills as a private investigator would help her to process. At last the day of reckoning felt near at hand.

Half-full
by Jack Parker

For the record, I'm generally a positive guy – glass half-full and all that. I mean, I've seen a lot of clouds, a lot, and I can assure you, if you look hard enough and long enough at them, even the really dark ones, you can find a little silver lining once in a while. Case in point, Tuesday, I was on the city bus heading downtown for another job interview when I picked up a crumpled newspaper that was only a couple of days old. Right there on the back, under the heading 'Wedding Announcements,' was Jill Thompson – my Jilly – standing arm in arm with some tall asshole in a turtleneck.

It was great to see her. Smiling up at me with that smile of hers, the real one that, when it was directed at you, I swear could almost make you believe in God. If that smile wasn't a silver lining I don't know what is. Gave me a good feeling about her the very first time I saw it. The cloud, of course, was standing next to her in a stupid sweater with neat little rows of perfect white teeth. It's not that I'm unhappy for her. Honestly. She's finally getting that 'long-term commitment' she's been so concerned with for all these years. Who wouldn't be? But *this* guy?

I tore the paper carefully down the middle to separate the happy couple and then ripped Turtleneck into small pieces and dropped him on the floor. Now cursing and stomping a piece of paper is not, and I am certain of this, the kind of thing that would be considered a parole violation. But in a world filled with camera phones and overly sensitive people, you just never know how the authorities might try to manipulate a little thing like that into some kind of evidence against you. Fortunately, getting back to the optimism I'm trying to tell you about, I was on the number seven downtown and you'd have to go monkey-shit bonkers and tear the roof off the bus to get a rise out of anybody there. So I settled back in my seat and was thrilled to see that Jilly's half of the wedding announcement included both the date and location of the upcoming festivities.

Four p.m. Saturday, the fourteenth at the Temple of Holy Serenity, reception to follow, blah, blah blah. I wasn't expecting an invitation or anything. But maybe I could stop by with a gift or something, show Jilly that I've moved on, you know? A little good will, bury the hatchet and all that – certainly nothing that would compromise the boundaries of a restraining order. Either way, I figured finding that paper was a good sign, and hey, I can read signs like no other.

When I got to the church on Saturday, the ceremony

had just ended. Jilly and Turtleneck, now dressed in a black tuxedo, were greeting guests as they moved from the chapel auditorium to the reception area. I got in the back of the line and only got a few nervous glances from the nosy people in front of me. Maybe I was sweaty and a little... untucked. But I challenge anyone to run nine blocks in a three-piece suit and rented shoes carrying a heavy goddamned box and look any better.

Now I won't deny that I spent the last few days imagining myself bursting through those chapel doors at the precise moment when the minister asks the audience if anyone has any objections to the marriage. I damn sure have a few. I made a list. But this isn't Hollywood. Even though I left my apartment early and looking pretty good I never really had a chance. The number twelve north-bound got stalled in traffic on account of a wreck at the corner of Warren and Lindsey. People can't drive for shit anymore, I can assure you of that. Teenagers texting and driving, old people who suddenly can't remember which pedal is the brake and which one is the gas, take your pick. I get my driving privilege restored in a couple of months but I'm in no great hurry to rejoin this group of idiots. The bus wasn't at a designated stop but I was eventually able to persuade the driver to bend the city's policy and let me out. I ran the last nine blocks. Sure I was late, but I made it.

When Jilly's eyes finally met mine I was still way back in the line. I'd imagined that moment for so long. That tiny instant of recognition. Of connection. I'd been practicing in the mirror. Unfortunately the look she returned did not measure up to my hopes. She looked surprised – I get that – but the look of surprise quickly changed to what one of fear. Fear of who? C'mon Jilly. It's me. I love you. I would never hurt you. I did my time. All that other bullshit is in the past. Today is about the future. I really wanted to tell her these things – but she was already shouting to someone in the reception hall. Right away three of the groomsmen came running through the side door one of whom was her asshole brother, Patrick.

I hadn't seen Patrick since the pre-trial hearing. Two years ago – maybe. At that time I had agreed, reluctantly, to drop the assault charges against him and he, in turn, dropped a criminal damage complaint against me over alleged vandalism done to his precious Subaru. The 'lawyers' at the public defender's office are worthless, believe me. I told the guy, there's no way they can link me, forensically, to Pat's car. No evidence whatsoever. It was all circumstantial at best. Plenty of people saw him pounding me though. But the PD was adamant that I not let it go to trial. Worried about my courtroom 'presence' in front of a jury. What the fuck is that supposed to mean?

Now here was Pat, weaving his fat ass around pews and people, talking on a cell phone. His face was red like his bow tie was cinched up a bit too tight. I figured he was calling the cops so I put the gift box down right where I was standing and bolted out the door onto Broadway.

I could have taken a cab, but I'm not exactly sitting on a gold mine these days, and when I rounded the corner onto Lindsey, the bus was just pulling away from the stop. I caught up to it quickly and started banging on the side. The driver hit the brakes – sometimes they do and sometimes they don't – and let me on. Nine blocks later I transferred back to the twelve southbound on Warren – different driver from earlier, thankfully – and didn't see any signs of anybody following me. I got off at Clairmont and walked the last few blocks west to 23rd Street. Lots of people were out but nobody seemed to be in a hurry – Saturday afternoon in springtime and all. I rounded that last corner and stopped. There were two police cars in front of my apartment building. Could've been a coincidence; the police come to my building a couple of times a week, at least. But I decided not to push it – even a streak of good luck has its limitations. Not that I was running away from anything. Running just makes you look like you might be guilty of something.

I continued walking west instead to 27th Street and dropped into Bruno's Deli. The sandwiches at Bruno's are fabulous and I hadn't eaten all day. I don't eat often but when I do, I prefer it to taste like it was prepared with human consumption in mind. Try that at the Chinese place across the street and see where it gets you. Besides, I knew Candace was working. Candace was one of Bruno's newest waitresses and, by far, the best. I've waited over an hour at lunchtime just to get a table in her area. She's always glad to see me and makes my water just the way I like it – quarter glass of ice, bottled water, squeeze of lemon – no wedge, no seeds, no excessive pulp – and never acts like I just asked her to build the goddamned pyramids or something. She's cute too, that Candace. Red hair, short, big smile – she reminds me a lot of Jilly in fact. If she changed her hairstyle and lost fifteen pounds she'd be a ringer.

Candace took my order and then stood by my booth and stared up at the television mounted above the counter. Some kind of a bomb threat downtown she told me in a serious whisper. Up on the screen was, without a doubt, the Temple of Holy Serenity. Two men in heavy leaded suits huddled behind an armoured vehicle. One of the men was looking through the doors of the chapel with a pair of binoculars while the other manipulated a small joy-stick controller. The television shot then shifted through the doorway and zoomed in on a stainless steel robotic device that was working its way jerkily around the gift box I'd left for Jilly. What a bunch of idiots. The reporter from the TV station was giving play-by-play commentary to the camera feed. He spoke in a hushed monotone. It was like watching a fucking golf tournament. By the time I finished my pastrami on rye the robot had x-rayed the box and loaded it into a large steel container mounted to a trailer and the bomb techs had driven off. The reporter informed us that the package was to be detonated at a secure, remote location. He made no effort to conceal his disappointment that nothing had blown up on camera. Then they put my picture on the screen. It was a few years old, but it was definitely me.

So now, here I am sitting in county lock-up. Evaluating, as I have a tendency to do, all the things that have happened since I found that newspaper on Tuesday. It would be easy to take a negative view of it all. Declare the glass to be half-empty. But I contend that, with a close examination of all the bits and pieces, the positive feeling I have right now is completely justified. I'm making a list.

1. Where am I? Well, I'm in the county jail, and jail sucks. I wouldn't try to tell you otherwise. The judge set my bail at $250,000 dollars. Seems a bit high, but he wasn't interested in my opinion. Innocent until proven guilty is one of those jokes that nobody in here laughs at. Either way it looks like I might be here a while, and I won't lie, it's hard in here. Physically hard. Everything is made of either concrete or steel. Even the toilet is made of steel and it doesn't have a seat to comfort your ass or a door to preserve your dignity. The mattress is about as thick as a slice of cheap sandwich bread. The pillow is a saltine cracker.

And the smell. All the times I've been here over the years the smell has never changed. The first thing that hits you is a combination of bleach and pine sol which never quite covers up the undertone created by a hundred years or so of whiskey-sweat, vomit and shit. It's a smell that works its way into your clothes and your hair. It flavours the food. But I contend that it could be much worse. They're holding back on some of the charges against me until after they autopsy the package I left at the church. The one they blew up. Federal charges could be pending. They're morons, of course, but in the meantime I've got my own cell. My own ten by ten steel palace. No drunks puking on my shoes. Nobody kicking my ass just to show someone else how tough they are. It really hasn't been too bad so far.

2.   What about the case against me? They say 'the truth shall set you free.' Well I say, and I want you to pay close attention to this, I say 'they' are a bunch of fucking schmucks. The only

thing you can count on to set you free from the U.S. legal system is reasonable doubt. Reasonable doubt and the truth have almost nothing to do with each other. The truth might get stuck to reasonable doubt's shoes once in a while, crossing the street. I'll take reasonable doubt over the truth every time. The x-ray taken by the bomb robot showed an unidentifiable mass at the center of the box surrounded by silverware. Silverware, it turns out, is a very common source of shrapnel in the construction of homemade explosive devices. This type of information is readily available on the internet and I'm not saying I haven't seen it myself. I've seen all kinds of things. I'm an insomniac. Surfing the web, however, does not make me the Unabomber. As I have pointed out to my attorney, another genius from the public defender's office, silverware is also one of the top ten most common gifts for newlyweds. Google it. As for bomb residue? Hello?, The bomb squad blew up the box. Wouldn't the residue inside the container be their own? It's not like they found any bomb making material in my apartment. It all seems to lead to only one conclusion – reasonable doubt. The truth. Well, maybe the truth is that what I put in the center of that box was not a bomb, but it would have ripped that reception hall apart in a way that no explosion ever could. Maybe I put photographs of Jilly in there instead. Photos of both of us. Lewd photos taken by young people who weren't thinking too much about the future. I figured including those photos would drive him away from her. Maybe they would have. But I realise now that even if they did, they wouldn't drive her towards me. So what's the point?

3.   What about the future? Believe me, the glass is still half-full. Finding that newspaper gave me the opportunity to finally deal with the past and put it behind me. A decade of therapy should be so productive. Whether I'm in here a week or a month or a year, I'm leaving a better person. And now, there's Candace. I've got a good feeling about

that girl. Saturday at Bruno's, when they put my picture on the screen, she knew it was me. She looked me right in the eyes and she knew, but her smile never wavered. She never asked me what I did or didn't do. When she went back to the kitchen I thought she might be calling the cops. But she came back instead with a refill for my coffee and a piece of apple pie. And, get this, she did not add the pie to my ticket. Nothing ever tasted better.

Sometimes the deputies let me make phone calls. It's supposed to be for lawyer bullshit but today I called Bruno's instead. Candace wasn't able to come to the phone but I'll try again tomorrow, like I said, I've got a good feeling about her.

POOL

by Aaron Malachy Lewis

I'm playing pool with June and her friend who keeps trying to be nice although I recognise her for the soul-suck moron she is even before she starts telling me about her multiple abortions. What is her name? Something that starts with an M. Maybe. The bar is humming with noise and there's a light out overhead, which gives the place a blurrier feel than usual. I'm standing with my back to June shoving a dollar into the jukebox so I can hear Eminence Front for the third time tonight when I hear a voice behind me that sounds familiar but not enough for me to react. I have another song to pick and I can't decide, and then that voice again, so I turn around. It's that older guy who knows June. He's usually sitting at the end of the bar with a giant tank of beer in hand and a bag of takeout near him. And now I get the feeling he's trying to pilot an inevitably doomed effort into her pants, but I can't be bothered. I'm back to scrolling through the list of songs when June's friend makes some comment about running, and I turn to her and laugh, saying something about how I need to start running because I feel huge as fuck, just joking, and his voice floats over to me, unsolicited.

'You're not even fat. You're skinny as hell.'

I swivel around now. He's standing, pool stick in hand. My pool stick? Probably. I've never actually looked at him before. He's really tall, with short dark hair that is combed to a small point at the top of his forehead, but he has really fine facial features that I find fascinating. Nose and cheekbones. He also has huge, bulging dark eyes and an earring in his left ear, very nineties. He's wearing what looks like waiter clothes, all black, and a jacket that's way too big for him and makes him look larger than he is. The way he's looking at me, slightly defiant, slightly curious, pisses me off.

'Sorry, who the fuck are you?' This barrels out of my mouth like a train.

Whatever he was expecting, it wasn't that. He keeps a grip on my pool stick as I take a step toward him, fencing myself between him and June. I don't know what I'd even be protecting her from, though. He's her fucking friend, acquaintance, whatever. He waits a long time before he speaks again.

'You just said you were fat, I'm just telling you, you're not.'

I squint up at him. 'Thanks for the validation.'

He looks like he's weighing his options. 'Sorry.'

'Whatever.'

He sets the cue down and heads toward the bar. I turn back to June. She sighs. 'That's just Tyler. You know Tyler.'

'Do I?'

She nods. 'Yeah. I met him a while ago. He works at that Italian place next door.'

I think for a minute. 'Classy one or shitty one?'

'I introduced you.'

'I was probably drunk.'

She gives me a look, but doesn't suggest I go apologise or anything. I go toward the bar, knowing I don't need another drink but wanting one anyway. I feel someone at my side suddenly, and of course.

'I'll get the next one,' Tyler says.

'Why?'

That confused look again. I don't know if it'll ever get old.

'Seems like I pissed you off earlier. Thought I'd make up for it.'

'Right.'

I sink into a seat, and he sits in the one next to me. I stare straight ahead. Adam makes the drink and looks at me, then at Tyler, then back at me again. My eyes flick in Tyler's direction, and Adam nods, setting the drink in front of me. I start swirling it automatically, clockwise, still not looking at him. He takes a huge dip into his litre of beer and studies me, I can tell by the way his eyes fall on the side of my face.

'So you're a friend of June's?'

'Yeah. You too?'

'Yeah, she's in a lot when I come here after work.'

I remember what June said, that his work is right next to the bar.

'I know, I'm usually with her,' I say. 'But strangely, I don't remember you.'

'How long have you known her?'

I clench my teeth. 'Longer than you have.'

He laughs at this, and I realise he's going to be just another old fuck who, for some reason, loves my mouth.

'Probably true. How'd you two meet?'

I hesitate. Dez's face floats into my mind. 'Through her old roommate.'

He thankfully doesn't question further, so I take this opportunity. 'Don't bother hitting on her.'

'What?'

'What did I say?'

He laughs again. 'Already tried, don't worry.'

Don't worry? Now I'm curious, so I turn to him.

'Yeah? How'd that work out for you?'

Funny, she'd never mentioned this part.

'About how you'd expect. She kept calling me to go out and then we'd just kind of sit in silence. Sometimes talking, not usually. Finally I asked her what the deal was, because let's face it, not many twenty-something year old girls call me up out of the blue to hang out, not unless they want something. And then she tells me, No, we're just friends. Like I was stupid for even thinking otherwise.'

The audacity of all of this throws me for a second. The way he volunteers this information so quickly and freely makes me uneasy. Where was I was on all these nights he's talking about?

'How old are you again?' I eye him.

'Thirty-eight. Why?'

He doesn't look thirty-eight. Thirty-five, maybe. More like thirty-three.

'Really?'

He looks flattered now. 'Yeah, why?'

'You just don't look it.'

'Thanks.'

I take a drink.

'How old are you?'

'Twenty-five,' I say.

'Sounds about right.'

'What does that mean?'

'I always seem to get twenty-year-olds. I don't know what it is. Been dating them for twenty years now. Twenty years of twenty-year-olds.'

I take another drink. This isn't dignified. Plus, what he's saying is making me feel gross. His hands are on the bar and I notice he wears two silver rings on his fingers too. Just like Dez.

'I'm not twenty.'

'Close enough.'

He laughs now. He'll be lucky if I don't break a pool stick over his face by the end of the night. I get up and walk back to June. He calls after me, and just then I realise I didn't tell him my name.

Someone decides we should all go out to smoke. Tyler takes up way too much room on the bench across from me, and June sits next to him, not too close. I'm stuck by the friend, whose name still escapes me. She asks me for a cigarette and I give her one of my girly ones. The ones that are all white and smell like marshmallows. I always have two different packs for this reason. Well, sometimes I like the girly ones too. Tyler smokes menthols. Gross. I resist the urge to cross my legs.

'My dad still has the pig farm out in Western Kansas. It's gone to shit though. Literally,' Tyler says.

June acknowledges this with a blink.

'When I was eight I had to kill a boar as big as a table with a .22. My dad just hands it to me, tells me to go shoot Killer. The fucking pig was called Killer. The damn thing just wouldn't die. I must have shot it a million times.' He taps a finger against his forehead. 'They all just bounced off that hard plate they have right here. My dad came out a half hour later and saw that I hadn't gotten the job done, so he just took an ax to him.' Tyler takes a drag.

'Jesus,' June's friend says.

'Yeah. I was eight. Then when I was twelve I had to artificially inseminate sows with a ketchup bottle. That was fun.'

I snort. 'Pig fucker.'

He grins. He thinks he's hot shit.

'Anyone want a drink?' He looks at my glass, then at me pointedly. 'I hate seeing empty glasses. Must be the waiter thing.'

I sigh. 'Fine.'

He stomps his cigarette, hocks a huge glob of phlegm into his empty cup, goes inside.

I look at June. 'Charming.'

She shrugs. 'What?'

'Your friends.'

She laughs. 'I know.'

I take the seat next to her, where Tyler was just sitting. I start playing with her hair, and she runs her fingertips, very lightly, over the side of my thigh. Her friend ignores us.

'Feeling okay?' I ask.

'Yeah.'

We're back inside. I've lost count of the glasses by now. Tyler is staring as he grips a pool cue.

'You're playing me next.'

I sway. 'Fine.'

The sinew on his forearms stands out as he chalks the stick, and I suddenly get the really bad feeling that he's going to slaughter me. He bends down and starts racking the balls.

'I used to play for money. In the nineties I got my kicks embarrassing frat boys at the bar up by campus.'

'Will you shut up?' I slur. The fucking nineties. 'I'm ninety-nine percent sure no one in this bar gives a fuck.'

I lean on my pool cue. I don't even know where June and her friend have gone. I bend down, trying to steady myself so I can break.

'You're holding it wrong.'

Everything is spinning slightly.

'Fuck you.'

He raises his hands as if in surrender, but I'm not stupid. I make a pitiful-ass break but I don't care. He sinks his next two shots. Shit. I bump him not so lightly on the way to make my next shot.

'If you lose, you have to fuck me,' I spit.

That dumbstruck thing again. His mouth might as well fall open.

'Fine.'

He hammers the balls into the pockets. One after the other. Boom boom boom. He finally biffs it and I sink a couple, not enough. Purple, blue, yellow. He just has the eight left. I know I'm fucked.

I storm out the back door before I even have a chance to see his face. I light a cigarette, the smoke floating away from me in wreaths. I hear the door and turn my head. He's walking toward me, lighting one of his shitty menthols.

'Levi.'

'No.'

He laughs, not in a mean way.

'Why are you mad?'

'If you really didn't want to fuck me you could have just said so.'

He gives me a strange look.

'That's not what you said.'

'That is exactly what I said.'

'You said if I win.'

'I didn't.'

He steps into my space. I barely come up to his chest. He shakes his head.

'You're nuts.'

I finally look up. 'What was your first clue?'

He laughs and holds my face. The softness surprises me. I reach up to ball the front of his work shirt in my fist. Am I trying to teach him a lesson? If it's that, or some fucked up kind of conquest, it should feel more like one. Just more of June's leftovers. No, more like rejects. That's all I am too, anyway. We all know it.

I pull him down toward my mouth.

I know I won't remember the walk to Tyler's house later. The sidewalk is uneven and I almost fall several times. At one point he grabs me under the arms just in time before I hit the ground. Vertigo.

'How much longer.'

'Like a hundred feet. Quit your bitching, kid.'

I say, 'Fuck you,' but I'm laughing.

The automatic flood light on his porch flicks on, almost blinding me. There's a ton of crap on his porch. An old dog crate, a couple folding chairs, a small rusty table in the shape of a hand, a swirl pattern in the center of its palm. I almost kick over a few stolen pint glasses that line the steps. The screen door has a huge hole in it that's patched with duct tape. Tyler drops his keys and I lean into him, pressing my face against his back for a moment before he gets the door open. He doesn't bother locking it.

The house is dirty, but what I notice first is the art. There is a huge green sectional couch in the living room, and above it are huge stretched canvases, four or five of them. There's a cubist piece, all blue and yellow and orange, and two huge surrealist paintings by the window. In both of them, the subject, which looks like Tyler's face, is being swallowed by its surroundings. In one of them there is a disembodied ear. The last one I see is a portrait that is too detailed. The girl's hair sweeps across her jaw and her half-smile is too real. I don't want her staring at me any longer, so I follow Tyler to the kitchen. It's full of stolen glassware, and I see labels from probably every establishment in town. He pours me some water in a cup that's from some Mexican restaurant and I take it. I can't stop looking at his earring. I wonder if it's ever been caught in anyone's teeth.

'That portrait,' I say.

'What?'

'That's your ex, isn't it.'

I watch his mind retreat as deep as the sea. Just for a moment.

'I almost married her.'

'Shame.'

I lean against him, pressing him back into the fridge. He's coming at my face again and I forget why I'm here and I don't care and he's picked me up and is carrying me into his room. He tosses me on the bed and I bounce before my ass hits something hard. I pull back the sheets and see a buck knife lying innocently against the mattress. I'm watching him take his shirt off when I see the rifle leaning against the wall in the corner, the boxes of ammunition on his bedside table, the four bags of rock salt against the dresser. He lights a cigarette, inside. Who is this person?

I pull a cigarette from my pack and he lights it for me, and I watch the smoke float to the ceiling. Before I've smoked the whole thing he pushes me down on the bed and kisses me again. I manage to kick the buck knife out of the way.

He somehow manoeuvres me onto my hands and knees, thank God. I don't want to see anything.

Commuter Community
by Ross Garner

Front carriage, 7.15am. So quiet before the rush. When we arrive at Edinburgh Waverley I'll be the first one off the train and through the gates. So quick before the crush.

I take the second seat on the right, next to the window. More leg room than a table seat, but no 'Priority' sign for old people, wheelchairs and bastards. Headphones in, ambient pop soundtrack on. Back to sleep.

But no rest. Got to wait for the ticket guy. My eyes are closed but my other senses tingle. With each passing commuter they flick open and then slip shut again. Angry happy man takes his seat ahead of me – so severe, but so happy when he meets someone he knows. Fat mole man moves to his end of the carriage – always relaxed, newspaper in hand. Skinny hair gel man sees someone sitting in his seat – moves away, eyes narrow. Normally he sleeps, but today he'll read. He's too annoyed now.

This is my commuter community, all in suits. No one would travel at this time unless they were wearing a suit.

I spend five hours a week with these people. That's why I've given them names.

The train begins to rumble. We're moving. A girl appears. She looks left, at the man in the aisle seat, bag by the window. He'll move if he's asked, but for now he pretends he's asleep. Not a regular. She looks at me. 'Mind if I sit here?' Horror. I recognise her from the day before. She sat beside me then as well.

'Not at all,' I say. I look back out the window.

'Weren't you sitting here yesterday?' she asks.

A question. My headphones are in, I can pretend I haven't heard. I look at her. 'Yes.' Headphones! I pull them out. 'Sorry, yes I was.'

'I didn't mean to interrupt.' She did. We both know she did.

'You didn't,' I lie. 'It's fine.' Angry happy man looks up. Angry? Not happy anyway. He wants to chat, and wishes the girl was sitting with him.

'Do you always sit in the same seat?' she asks.

'When I can,' I say, like some neurotic thunder twat.

The wider community have noticed the disruption. Their eyes are drifting towards us. Angry happy man is angry. Fat mole man is on edge. Skinny hair gel man has lowered his book. They know it's not my fault, but they blame me nonetheless.

'Why?' she asks.

'We all do,' I say.

'Who?' she asks, spitting out staccato questions that mean I'll never be able to sleep.

'All of us, on this train. We have our seats.'

Skinny hair gel man looks horrified. I've revealed our secret, our unacknowledged truth. Tomorrow morning we're all going to take a different train, or at least a different carriage. It's the only way. The equilibrium is ruined.

'Would you mind if this seat was mine?'

I stare at her, aghast, a pleasant smile plastered over my face. 'Not at all,' I say.

A familiar voice, female but not human, echoes through the carriage: 'The next stop is Croy.'

'My stop,' says the girl. She stands, shoulders her bag, smiles again. 'See you tomorrow.'

She gets off the train and I watch her go, afraid to return to the community. I know that it would be best if I just stood up, slipped quietly through to another carriage. But that'll disrupt the system, and I'll get stuck in the crowd at Waverley.

I turn round slowly, closing my eyes as if everything is normal, and see Fat mole man talking to skinny hair gel man. They're smiling. Ahead of me, angry happy man is watching me. He smirks and looks back out the window.

I look out the window as well, and my eyes meet angry happy man's reflection. He looks back at me.

'She liked you,' he says, smirking.

I laugh and make myself more comfortable. Back to sleep.

Trigger Happy
by Syd Briscoe

'C'mon then, show me what you got!'

The kid crows across the bar, shaggy dog hair hanging in his face and his slurred words in an American drawl as a much bigger man takes offence and lunges for him. Everything is broken glass and sticky tables and shitty mullet rock whining from the jukebox, and I'm starting to get a headache.

I have a bad feeling about this, getting on for Obi-Wan levels of foreboding. I'm all for scoping out this kid before we decide whether to invite him to join our group, but I'm not getting a good feeling from him here. This is a *kid*, he can't be older than twenty.

A kid who puts cigarettes out on himself for the hell of it, or that's what Elvis said he saw, but a kid nonetheless.

A dog that doesn't know to get out of the way when a car's headed for it, that's dangerous. A mad dog who chases cars until one hits it, that's really dangerous. Seems like this kid has been chasing cars for a long time.

'I'm gonnae kill you, you wee bastard.'

Whoever large'n'scary number one is, he's confident enough in his ability to squash the kid flat that he's shouting about it to the whole bar. I watch Old Elvis sigh through his fat nose and take another sip of his pint, melted-cheese Weegie face rippling under the dim overhead light. This is supposed to be strictly recon, just the old man pointing out the fresh blood and me having a look to make sure I recognise him, so I can keep a watch out. I really don't want to have to deal with this drama. It's supposed to be my day off.

'Piece of cake,' Elvis said. 'Have a few drinks, keep an eye on the guy and just see what you can see. Nae bother.'

I'm going to kill Elvis. 'Kill me, huh? Big talk from a big man.' It's the voice that catches attention. Those bland mid-Atlantic vowels that make everything sound like a line from a movie. That's why a lot of people are looking at him when it happens.

Without warning, the kid produces a knife from somewhere on his person and slashes it across his own forearm.

Elvis moves for his jacket, but like the rest of the bar he's frozen as blood drips and the kid starts to laugh at the big man's face. A shattered sound, like he's been deepthroating broken bottles. The man who'd been threatening him a moment ago now looks like he's fallen through a trap door and ended up in front of Satan himself.

'C'mon then, let's go. I got *all* day.'

The kid throws his arms wide with a sneer, drops of

blood spattering on the floor in a lazy arc around him. It's triumphant. Mad, but triumphant.

Looks like Elvis was right; he is our brand of crazy. Maybe not everyone's cup of tea, but he could be our eighth shot of tequila.

'You're fuckin' mad.'

The big guy's white as a sheet, babbling in a heavy Glasgow murmur. He grabs his friend's shoulder and tugs at it, wanting to bolt.

'You're mental, you are.'

'Ten minutes ago you were the one shovin' me outta your way. Still wanna fuck with crazy?'

He laughs again, and it's a childish sound. Gleeful. There's a manic glint in his eye that promises this is far more interesting than just a bar fight. This isn't just drunken bravado. The kid's enjoying himself.

'Man,' the kid chuckles. 'You're the one who wanted to whip 'em out and measure. Your fuckin' turn.'

I watch transfixed, not even glancing to see Elvis's reaction, as the kid flips the knife over in his hand with practiced ease and holds it out to the other man, handle first. The big guy backs away from him like he's infectious, not like he's offering him a weapon.

Fear is a greater weapon than the little throwing knife the kid's holding could ever be, and he knows it.

'You're fuckin' insane.'

The kid just smirks, like there isn't blood running down his arm, dripping through his fingers onto the dirty floor. Like there isn't a bar full of people staring at him like he's the antichrist.

He smirks and stares and doesn't fucking blink and there's *nothing* behind his eyes. After a few seconds it's too much for the big guy, who grabs his friend's shoulder again and hauls him to the door.

'Fuck this.' I hear as they pass us, bar staff as invisible as the wallpaper. 'No' going near that nutter. Fuckin' rabies or something.'

The kid just laughs again, wearily this time, and drops down on a seat at the bar. He pulls a bandana from his pocket to wrap around his bleeding arm; this clearly isn't his first rodeo. The other patrons slowly go back to their drinks. Everyone's too afraid or just doesn't care enough to ask him to leave, now the show and the excitement is over. It's not like this kind of thing doesn't happen around here.

He orders another drink as if nothing's happened, asking for unspecified beer in that Sometown USA accent. I don't give him Tennent's. I get the feeling that's not what he means when he says 'beer'.

'You okay? That was a nasty cut.' I talk quietly as I fish a bottle of Budweiser out of the fridge. Elvis stays mum. Apparently sweet-talking the newbie is my job, this time. I decide to go the concerned route, rather than flirting. Choose your own adventure; don't turn to page three.

'Yeah... Sorry about the mess. I'll mop it up if you want.' He looks genuinely sheepish, and it's so out of place with what just occurred that I can't help but twitch a smile. That cornfed American look on his face, like Jett Rink before money ruins him. He could be James Dean if he cut his hair.

'That's alright. It's pretty quiet right now, I've got time.'

I put his beer in front of him and he starts peeling the label off before he even takes a swallow. His fingernails are so bitten down they look like he's stuck his fingers in a pencil sharpener. I wonder how he can stand to touch anything without flinching.

'What's your name?'

'Robbie.' He doesn't offer anything more, but that's all I need.

'It's good to meet you, Robbie.' I gesture to Elvis, sitting a few chairs away in his usual spot.

'This is a friend of mine. Elvis. I think you two would get along. It seems like you've got a lot in common.'

The kid looks confused, but he nods, glancing at Elvis's candle wax face curiously. He's hooked in enough by the oblique suggestion to go over and say hello, at least. The old man can handle the rest.

My part done, I take myself off to clean up the spilt blood. Whatever the group is up to, I still can't lose my job. I'm not going back to working in the pretzel shop in the bottom of the Buchanan Galleries even if that means mopping up other people's blood on a Wednesday night. Even if that means sweet-talking kids into putting themselves in danger.

With a terminal illness, they always say that you feel fine right up until the point that you don't.

The gun club was my terminal illness. It was fine, right up until the point it wasn't.

Robbie was the point it wasn't.

Robbie was the beginning of the end.

Point Blank
by Jane R Martin

Jenny was lonely after her daughter moved out. He wouldn't let her have a dog or cat. She wasn't interested in a gerbil or a fish. She knew she was starting to lose it when she felt affection for the stink bugs that took up residence in her home. She fancied she could tell them apart and felt a tug of sadness when she inevitably found one, legs up, most often on the mantle or in the bathroom sink. So, when Ben grinned at her on his side of the counter at the diner where she worked, she grinned back. And, when he dug her car out of the snowbank so she could get home, well, that was it. He said it was lonely in his house, too.

Jenny hadn't seen Ben since word of their affair got to his wife and exploded their world. *Note to self,* she thought, *you should have told him not to text you and leave his phone on the kitchen countertop.* She walked along the river's edge instead of using the paved hiking trail to avoid being seen because she knew everyone in a ten block area. The word was out that she had cheated and everyone in the mostly Irish-Catholic neighbourhood probably wanted to hang her naked, feet-first from the Tyler-McConnell Bridge with a nice big red 'A' tattooed on her ass. Short, compact, young looking for her fifty years, Jenny couldn't stop thinking of Ben as she walked towards their meeting place at the river. She poked her red hair behind her ears as she walked in short, nervous steps, face drawn, lips pressed tight. Early afternoon as she hurried to the bend in the river where they'd agreed to meet. The third cold, grey day in a row. She was sure the sun was shining where she was headed. She'd stopped at the bank and emptied the savings account; swiped, she acknowledged to herself. Larry would eventually drink it anyway. It was go now. Or stay. Go nuts or die. If her husband found her and Ben before they bolted, there would be such a blood bath that her life would end up as a biopic on the Lifetime Movie Network.

She reached the bend in the Brandywine where they'd first kissed. The sleepy river spread out as it wrapped around a tiny island (really a clump of dirt and one scrawny weeping willow) making wide ripples. Pebbles scrubbed the water clean, and the banks were lined with the dried-out remnants of last summer's nettles, oat grass, milkweed and goldenrod. A faithful pair of Canada geese floated past, paddling in unison with the current, breaking up the thin slices of ice. Jenny surveyed the river and thought of how much she had loved it in each and every season her entire life. Her roots dug deepest at the river. Her biggest regret was she couldn't pour it in her car. The river had always been there for solace and joy... long before Ben.

She stared downstream at the defunct mills on the banks of the river. Speculators had plans to turn the crumbling rubble into expensive loft condos. Very modern. No one in the neighbourhood could figure out who could afford to buy them. She wondered if the developer would block access to her river. *It doesn't matter.*

More than two hundred years ago, a munitions company set up shop on the banks of the river in Wilmington, first making gunpowder, morphing slowly from gunpowder to nylon stockings and then to chemical colossus. In the Trolley Square neighbourhood, textile plants lined the river, and a few scant blocks from the river, neat rows of brick houses were left from the days when shift workers walked home by the thousands from the plants. This was her turf. Hers. When she married thirty years ago, she moved into a red brick row house two blocks away from the red brick row house she grew up in. The area got trendy in the eighties and nineties and property values soared. Coach bags and Rolex watches appeared on the arms of those who walked the neighbourhood. Then the chemical giant laid off workers by the thousands. The textile factories closed and jobs moved to China, Bangladesh, and India. More recently, window boxes, large terracotta planters, and cherry trees that lined the streets could not hide plummeting housing prices. The 'For Sale' and 'Rooms to Let' signs littered the streets with reality. There was an ad campaign that ran in the eighties: 'Wilmington, the place to be somebody.' Flipped to fit the times: 'Wilmington, the place to be nobody.'

Jenny remembered when the five o'clock whistle blew and she heard the scrape of the men's boots on the pavement, the thwack of a ball as the kids played stickball, and the mothers' chorus yelling, 'Dinner!' from the stoops. She could see her husband as he made it up the crest of the hill with his lunch pail rhythmically thumping his thigh. That was when Larry was Larry, before the layoffs began. When Larry was handed his pink slip seven years ago, he never got off the bar stool to look for a job. His drunken rages suffocated the three of them. Her daughter Kathleen got her own place and Jennie hunkered down with the stink bugs.

She figured it was two or three days drive to Nebraska. If they kept to back roads, and didn't use credit cards or Easy Pass, they would be hard to trace. Larry wouldn't look for them in Nebraska, because who in Delaware even knew where Nebraska was? She'd heard Omaha was a good place to land. She needed a city, not some prairie town stuck among the cornstalks and feed lots. They had been planning for months. She figured she could find a waitressing job at a diner. She was a crackerjack waitress, not a bad grill cook, and after working for the catering company she could make omelettes for forty without breaking a sweat. Ben had been in touch with the Omaha police department and the chief said he'd talk to him. If that didn't pan out, he could always find work doing carpentry. He was so talented with his hands. She could see their future. They would live in a little house on the west side of town near the Platte River, the house would be a stone ranch that wasn't attached to another house, with a patio in back and a gas barbeque grill. Their families would blend and the kids would come for long visits. Someday their grandchildren would play on the grass and Ben would hang a swing from a tree.

She had done her research and, while the Missouri River was a mighty river and worthy of respect, the Platte River was most like her beloved Brandywine. The photos she found on the internet showed a wide, shallow river with low banks, no rocks and many small islands. The Platte would be her new river and she and Ben would plant new roots. They would splash in the river in summer and maybe skate on it in winter, during fall and spring they would watch as the sandhill cranes flew overhead on their eternal circular migrations north and south. She blinked and then she saw him. He was walking towards her but the day was so dim that she couldn't see his face. For a second she felt weightless. As he came closer, she was hit by the familiar rush she got whenever she was with him. Well-muscled, brown hair cropped close, he didn't look fifty-six. She loved his blue eyes. Then, she saw the look in his eyes, her pace slowed until her feet planted in the frozen packed dirt. He came to her, his arms at his sides, his hands clenched into fists,

'I can't go with you. It's all falling apart here. My son won't talk to me. My daughter hates me.'

Her mother raised Jenny to face things head-on. She spun her mind. *Do not stop. Do not feel anything.* No time for that. Eleven hundred miles to go. She saw her car speeding on the Pennsylvania Turnpike, then Route 80. It would take her longer without a second driver. She'd be on the road in an hour. She'd stay in Lancaster or Harrisburg and make *Pittsburgh* by tomorrow night. Then on to Toledo, Chicago or Davenport, depending on how tired she was. Then Omaha. At least four nights in hotels. She had the cash for hotels, meals, and gas.

'Jenny, did you hear me?'

His voice swung her back to the river and reality. She would not beg.

'Say something,' he said.

Her mind was screaming, *I gave up my life, as miserable as it was, for you. I stole money for you... for us.* She stamped her feet down hard to shove her feelings into her feet where she couldn't feel them. She couldn't go back to where she was and she had nowhere else to go.

He took her arm, 'Please say something. Say anything. I know you think I'm a chickenshit schmuck. We can leave later after things quiet down. We won't have to hide.'

She wrenched away from him, 'There's nothing to say. You've made up your mind. I've made up mine – I'm going. There's no way we can go on as before.'

'You're still going?' he asked, his eyes opened wide.

Jenny stuck out her chin, 'Yep, I'm going.'

'What about your daughter?'

'Kathleen is twenty-six years old, and she's seen what her father turned into. If I can start over, at least she'll have one parent she can be proud of.'

'I can't believe you're going without me. Is this it for us?'

'*You're* the one who decided not to go. We planned this.'

'Oh honey, I know we planned it. We didn't expect Monica to read my text. That was stupid of me. Once it all blew up, I didn't expect my kids to go so nuts. Please give me some time.'

She stared at him. He didn't get it. 'I don't *have* time. He's drunk, depressed, pissed and he's coming for me. I'm scared and I'm running.' She turned away from Ben and started walking fast. The last thing she heard was him yelling, 'Wait!' Yep, she'd be in Pittsburgh tomorrow. She walked as fast as she could then ran, her mind going faster than her feet. I'm packed, she thought, and the car is loaded. She shivered as the wind off the river cut her. She pulled her scarf up around her ears. He *was* a chickenshit schmuck. Coward. They all were when it came down to it. He was all mister romance at the start. She had to keep running. She realised she hadn't packed her warmest boots. Too late. She couldn't drive by her house and risk seeing Larry. *Okay*, she thought, *Ben wasn't a total chickenshit schmuck.* He was nice. Too nice. Word of his affair had toppled him from the top step of the altar on which his kids worshipped him. As a cop he fixed things, and their affair wasn't going to be an easy fix. Time for her to move on. Her daughter's response when she told her that morning was, 'I'm surprised you didn't do it years ago. Go for it.' Kathleen wouldn't tell Larry where her mother went. She knew better. So, it was go with the plan and hit the road. She had really screwed up. Ha. She had. When had an affair fixed a problem? She was stupid to start the whole thing. She got caught up in it like Dorothy getting caught up in the tornado. Jenny got it in her head that Omaha was Oz. Only she hadn't planned to land alone. No wicked witch in the east or west or whichever direction the broomstick came from. No good witch either. Definitely no good witch. Just her, on her own, trying to make a living and trying to get over Ben. It wasn't going to be easy because he really got inside her. Ha. No, he did. He opened her up like a can opener and poured her out like a can of soup into a hot pot. He was hot alright. Her chest hurt and she was freezing. She slowed to a walk. Her car was just around the corner. What if Larry had found her car? *I need to be ready to run*, she thought. Damn. Damn. Damn him and his drinking. Damn him and his ugly, angry mouth. Damn it that things never, ever, work out. She turned the corner and scanned the area to see if Larry was waiting. No, she didn't see him. She hit the remote and reached for the handle of her car door. She heard the sound of someone one running. She turned, her heart beating fast. Ben caught up with her, running flat out, too out of breath to talk. She didn't know whether to smile or cry, only that hope, that terrible affliction for the miserable, stirred inside her.

'I can't let you leave,' he gasped.

For a moment they were suspended, drifting towards each other. Then, Larry was there. Jenny's brain screamed, *Where did he come from?* Her world sped up and slowed down at the same time. Larry. Gun. Shock. No. Time. *Oh, God, he's brought his father's Luger from the Second World War!* Larry aimed the ancient firearm directly at her. She thought that if he fired the old thing, they would probably all blow up. Ben stepped in front of her and lunged at Larry. When Larry stepped back and took aim again, Ben charged again. Their hands locked on the gun as they struggled. The barrel kept pointing back at Jenny as if she were true north. She stood frozen to the spot, and she thought Larry's mind had derailed, and she knew booze and adrenaline had fuelled his rage. She watched as Ben played his cop role, measuring, estimating the danger and trying to figure an out. Three pair of eyes riveted on the barrel of the gun as it aimed at her again and was shoved off target. As the two men grappled, she saw their arms begin to shake. She thought of the word 'cuckolded' and understood Larry's need for revenge for what she had done to him. The reason she did it didn't matter. She had humiliated him in front of everyone he knew. She stepped closer to the men, Ben said, 'Don't. I've got this. Run.' But instead, she yanked Larry's arm, 'Please, please Larry. Don't do this, even if

I deserve it. Don't do this to our daughter after what I've already done.' Larry's movements slowed. 'I'll go and you can tell everyone whatever you want about me. No one will blame you. If you give up the gun, you can go on with your life. Kathleen, think about Kathleen.'

He said, 'I could kill you.'

She said, 'I know. I deserve it. But you don't. Kathleen doesn't. Let me go. I won't bother you again. You won't even notice I'm gone. You'll be relieved.' She watched as he paused, his eyes glazed with booze. He shifted a little and the hand holding the gun started a slow descent to his side. Ben said nothing, waiting, and then reached and gently unfolded the gun from Larry's fist. Jenny and Ben locked eyes. Then Ben looked around and made sure there was no one watching who could be called as a witness. He pointed to her car and nodded for her to leave. He put his arm around Larry and said, 'Okay, I'm keeping the gun, this never happened, and I'm going to walk you home. Jenny is going for a drive to cool off.'

Jenny lurched the three steps to her car, the shock beginning to wear off and the panic starting to rise as the reality of what happened ricocheted off her nerves. As she opened the car door, her hand was shaking, then her legs started, and then she was on the ground crying and hugging herself. When she looked up, both men were gone from sight.

She sat for a moment to calm down. She repeated to herself that it was over and she was okay. Finally, she rose to her feet and got into her car. She started the engine, put the car into 'drive,' and pressed down on the accelerator. The calm voice of the GPS talked her through the haze and she was half way to the Pennsylvania Turnpike before she realised she had taken all of Larry's money and she didn't know if Ben would follow her. Her foot came off the gas. She was suspended on the highway for a moment, and then she lowered her foot back on the gas pedal. She kept driving. The first thing she would do was get a puppy. Stink bugs make lousy pets.

OCCUPIED SAN FRANCISCO
by Laura Boss

The couple upstairs have the best view in the entire building. They moved into the penthouse while I had my back turned for a moment. It is their first home. Had I known Mrs Sanford was going to sell I would have bought it myself. She knew I had been waiting years for the top floor. The old cow sold it out from under me in spite.

I see them in the building lobby: white-toothed, slim and golden-haired. They are obviously the kind of people to have a marble-clad fireplace, a row of French windows opening onto a balcony and high coved ceilings. I'm sure they have long white sheer curtains that blow with the breeze coming across the bay when the windows are open and that the light from the fire not only warms them as they sit curled around each other on the sofa sipping wine, but also highlights the brass ornamentation and brings the marble to a rosy glow. The elevator button for their floor is marked 'P' for penthouse and it shines more brightly than the other buttons.

They wake every morning at 7am, no doubt woken by the soft chime of one of those 'Zen' alarm clocks. He leaves her dozing in the linen sheets for an extra few minutes, kisses the back of her neck, and pads across the floor to the kitchen where he makes her a cappuccino with non-fat milk – a little coffee heart inscribed in the rich foam. He brings it to her in bed, where she is now sitting up, the creamy silk strap from her negligee sliding casually down her tanned shoulder as she reaches up to accept the cup. He pulls the thick velvet curtains open and the cool morning sun slides across the intricate parquet flooring. Another fucking perfect day.

She slips on her Lululemon yoga wear and walks with him to the corner. When he boards the Google bus she waves and blows a little air kiss. She checks her iPhone for messages and walks to the Yoga Tree, blonde ponytail swaying, *tra la, tra la*, for a morning stretch followed by gossip over a second non-fat cappuccino, without the little heart, at Starbucks. They are trying to get pregnant and she believes yoga will prevent stretch marks, erase labour pains and ensure she doesn't look fat until her sixth month at least. Yoga will guarantee that the baby is good-looking and a genius. Yoga is *wonderful*!

He is going to surprise her with a puppy. It will be pedigree, hypo-allergenic and house-trained. They will name it Max or Lucy and practice being parents. She will buy it organic kibble and educational toys at that little dog boutique on Sacramento Street and teach it to beg and roll over on command. They will take it with them to Telluride and Maui and post cute photos on Facebook. The Penthouse unit is allowed pets.

I see them in the window of the little neighbourhood cafe that is impossible to get into. I see her in the bookstore looking at postcards, a little *moue* of confusion between her lightly plucked brows. I see him on his phone crossing the street, on his phone in line at the drugstore and on his phone in the elevator, pushing 'P.' He blocks the doors and looks straight ahead as if there is no one else in the elevator listening to every word he says.

THE BUS RIDE
by Marie C Sanchez

While you and your friends were opening the Dubai comedy night at the Soho Bar and Grill, where it was rumoured that Robin Williams would drop in, I was walking the aisle of a bus in Puerto Vallarta, Mexico, following my cousin Lola. Have you ever been there, or in one of those tropical towns in Latin America where the buses are crucial forms of transportation and the colours are vivid and intense, the noises too loud, potholes too jarring, and the bus itself too crowded and everything is alien to life as we know it, at least my life in the Upper West Side with its quiet Honda Prelude, smooth ride low to the ground? Where buses double as entertainment forum and food court?

Lola gabs continually as we rumble towards my mother's house, where she's recovering from heart surgery. You, Allen, without family responsibilities, what do you know from taking buses to recovering mothers? And my God, Robin Williams? What would he think of the pork tamales we buy off the ten-year-old ferrying that steaming white plastic bucket, saying his mother had not even ten minutes ago lifted them from the pot? What of the gum, candies and roasted nuts for sale from the itinerant vendors who hop on and off freely after hitting up each of the chatting passengers for exactly one mile?

Understand Allen, these buses come every five minutes to run their routes Al, every five minutes. At every corner, and for less than fifty cents a ride! They take you everywhere Al.

Did Robin with his high velocity humour say that Dubai was 'so last year' and Abu Dhabi was *the* place now? What would he think of my music promoter Lola spending all our change in tips for the street musicians serenading us on the bus? Did he try new jokes about wars and deserts to fit the edgy vibe of the night? Did you laugh and howl and glimpse the full moon?

I would have liked that too, to be free in New York among you lovers of irony, especially with my disdain of fads. Instead, there's enough droll oratory and music here to satiate Lola: singers with and without instruments, solos, duos, trios. Comedians, too, without bite, and satirists, all vocalizing at the top of their lungs, flaunting, filling the bus. And always, the stained hand or grimy cap for tips.

One every five minutes, Al. I have the tickets to prove it. I recall my first time, not in Vallarta but in Guadalajara, which is similar but more like spring instead of summer.

I was heading to Lola's with bags of vegetables, lots of them. After making my way down the aisle several stops ahead of my own – I was so nervous – I waited and pressed the red ALTO button. I stepped off, the heavy bags swung me off balance, and I felt my ankle give, falling onto the concrete, vegetables flying everywhere, and the bus roared off, and on the ground, I bent forward to catch the rolling squash and oranges and cabbages while a few passersby gave me pitying looks.

I tried to write that Guadalajara story but was blocked by the black ache in my ankle and a loathing of weakness and vulnerability, without even a mention of the immaculate two-year-old looking serenely at me and my bags from over his mother's shoulder in the seat in front.

This time, there's a young man so good with his guitar that Lola gives him her card.

What's left? We exited on Avenida Constitucion, arrived as Mother was falling asleep from sedatives and waited. Dad was holding mom's hand. I sat on a chair against the wall.

That's when I had a chance to think of Soho, of you and your friends. Picture my dad's calloused hand holding an onion-papery one. Picture a young man with a banged-up guitar and dark tenor. Picture steaming pork tamales. A two-year old completely still, looking at you from long dark lashes for a long moment during the jarring, lively, jostling ride through life.

And this laughter edged with anger and despair, Al, this aching juxtaposition, this full-measured pause in the ride.

A Loving Family And A Forgiving God

by Gordon Legge

First stop after the High Street, next again left after that, the barber's.

He showed the barber his photos.

The barber fashioned a cut.

'Nicely done,' he said. 'Just the job,' he said. 'Nothing fancy.'

He left the barber a little something for himself.

Back out on the main road, to be exact its other side, a tattoo parlour.

He showed the tattooist his photos.

The tattooist inked the designs.

'Nicely done,' he said. 'Just the job,' he said. 'Nothing fancy.'

He left the tattooist a little something for himself.

He decided to call himself – Havoc.

Havoc took a single decker – a No. 30 – all the way down to Newcraighall.

He was looking for clothes, the best he could afford.

No way was he to scrimp. What you put on yourself was like what you put in yourself. It had to be quality. No point otherwise. You might as well…

Havoc found a shop.

He showed the assistant his photos. The assistant was younger than Havoc. Havoc called the assistant 'Big Man'.

'Big Man' kitted him out.

'Nicely done,' said Havoc. 'Just the job,' said Havoc. 'Nothing fancy.'

He left the assistant a little something for himself.

Havoc was tired: he was thinking as though he hardly had time to think, walking as though he hardly had time to walk. It didn't help that Newcraighall was all couples, folk with money. Havoc was still to get a job, a job and a wife. He would take what he could get. Persistence was key.

On the way back into town, he decided no – no he wouldn't call himself Havoc. Meerkats didn't name themselves. People didn't name themselves either.

And at that, he called it a day.

Tomorrow, early doors, he'd board a five and head on up to what was known locally as 'Holy Corner', but what Drunken Uncle Duncan called 'The Sweet Spot'. There, eventually, he'd 'come to terms with the grace and the glory of all that passes understanding'.

But first things first.

'Just pick one,' Drunken Uncle Duncan said. 'Just introduce yourself, then show them the photos, and tell them how you want to learn to concentrate. They're good at that. Trust me, they can help you. That's what they do.'

Split Decision
by Kev Sherry

It was an average working class street in Streatham, the rows of semi-detached houses separated by small gardens and wooden fences. Distant traffic hummed and buzzed along side streets like a secret generator powering London town while around corners children kicked footballs into the paths of older couples walking in the sunshine. The late afternoon sun felt cool on my face. Strands of cloud hung low over the city's skyline as I stopped at the foot of the garden path. This was the address.

A young man opened the door. His skin was darker than Gina's but there was no mistaking the face. I knew instantly it was one of her brothers. It was clear by his look of surprise that he knew who I was too.

'Hi, I'm looking for Gina? I'm Joseph.' I extended my hand. He took it, with some hesitation.

'Andry,' he said.

Andry was the youngest son – the brother directly above Gina. A good few years older than I, he was muscular, thin and wearing a white T-Shirt with an acid house smiley face imprint and brown canvas shorts. I could see elements of Gina in the curve of his eyebrows and the arch of his nose but he didn't share her red hair. His was also cropped short but dark brown in colour to match his skin.

'What d'you want, man?'

'I need to find your sister. I owe her an apology.'

He stared and nodded. 'Yeah, you do. She ain't here.'

I'd gone straight to Gina's place in West Hampstead when I got off the plane but there was no one there. I'd left my suitcase and bag sitting in the hall outside her flat. They would only slow me down. I knew her family lived in Streatham. That was my only clue. I went to an internet café to search through it for all the Falconers who lived in Streatham. There were three. I was first time lucky.

Andry was darker than Gina and his bare arms were toned and muscled. He could do some real damage with those things. I looked at the ground then stared past him into the hallway as Gina's dad came walking towards us, his shock of bright red hair and pale white, freckled skin in complete contrast to that of his son. He too was of a lean, sinewy, physique which his advancing years hadn't robbed him of yet. I'd seen him once, in London when he came to meet Gina briefly before our gig that night. The band had waved an awkward hello from around the table of the café we were eating in. He had seemed shy. He was about my height. Not tall, not small. I guess Gina got her height from her mother.

'It's you, is it?'

'Hi Mr Falconer.'

'You better come in I suppose. I'll make you a cuppa.'

The three of us sat in the kitchen waiting for the kettle to boil. It wasn't awkward at all. Andry stared at me as I tried to keep my eyes occupied by glancing around the small linoleum covered kitchen with its porcelain ducks hanging on the faded cream wallpaper. None of us knew what to say. Mr Falconer put down a cup in front of me. I was too scared to tell him I didn't take milk in my tea. I drank it anyway, and surprisingly found that I liked it. After all the strange places I'd been in the last few months there was a reassuring comfort to be found sitting in a small semi-detached house in the UK with a cup of tea in front of me – even if the company felt vaguely hostile.

I thought about trying to explain some of what I'd been through. I thought about getting idealistic. I thought about it and looked at the two of them sitting at the kitchen table with their tea, waiting for me to say something and it occurred to me they weren't the kind of guys who would tolerate my pseudo-intellectual nonsense.

Mr Falconer broke the silence.

'It's unexpected, having a pop star round at the house.'

I shifted uncomfortably in my seat.

'I liked your album. I'm more of a Motown man

meself. But I fought yer songs were good.'

'Thanks.'

'I fought it was shit,' Andry said grinning in what appeared to be a challenge of sorts.

There was silence as both men sized me up and waited for a response. I had no idea how I was supposed to react. They turned to one another and laughed and I squeezed out a relieved smile.

'What are you doing here, son?'

'I need to see Gina. This whole thing was a giant misunderstanding.'

I had to build bridges with these guys if I ever wanted to fix things with Gina. I ransacked my memory for things we may have in common.

'She's talking about quitting the music business. That your doing?'

I nodded. 'Kind of. But it was a mistake. If she quits the music business I'm quitting as well. I don't want to do it without Gina as my manager.'

'From what I heard, she was a bit more to you than a manager.'

I squirmed. 'Yup. I… care about her.'

Andry and Mr Falconer looked embarrassed by this frank and unnecessary admission. I could feel my cheeks going red. I was back at school and had embarrassed myself in front of the class. I had asked a girl out and she said 'no'. I was fourteen years old and was caught jerking off over the picture of Beyoncé by my pop music-hating friends.

'Can you let Gina know I came by?' I said, finishing my tea in one large gulp.

Manliness was called for. My inner voice was screaming at me to get up, to leave. The part of me that needed to see Gina managed to over-rule it. I couldn't slither away like the coward I always was. Gina wouldn't act like that. I tried to remember everything Gina had told me about her family.

'Gina told me you guys are boxers?'

'Yeah. Amateur boxers. Just for fun these days,' said Andry.

Mr Falconer interjected, 'Don't let this one fool you. He could've been professional... if he'd applied himself.'

Andry scowled, hearing this from his father, no doubt, for the umpteenth time.

'You ever box?' he asked me.

I still can't believe I was stupid enough to say yes. I knew nothing about boxing other than what I'd seen in Rocky movies. I think, somewhere deep in my brain, was the idea that this could be a male bonding thing. And by deep in my brain, I mean the really shallow part of the brain that houses the male ego.

'Take him out back and show him where we train,' Mr Falconer said.

On the paving stones that covered the backyard were fading painted lines in the shape of a boxing ring. Inside the little wooden shed, pressed up against the high, grey brick wall at the back of the yard was everything an amateur boxer could wish for. Training equipment, skipping ropes, punching bags and headgear hung from the sides of the hut. A weight bench took up all the floor space in the centre.

'She never told me you boxed.' Mr Falconer said.

'Only a bit in school and at uni,' I heard myself lie, my mind throwing out telepathic arms to try and pull the foolish words back into my mouth. I lifted a pair of gloves from the wall and for some reason weighed them in my hands then pulled one of them on. The glove felt heavy and comforting as it slid over my soft hands.

'Careful there,' said Mr Falconer, 'Andry might challenge you to a few rounds if you're not careful. He hasn't had a sparring partner in a while.'

Andry laughed and taking the gloves off me turned to his dad,

'Don't give him any ideas.'

'No,' I shouted, it came out unexpectedly and there was nothing I could do about it.

'That sounds like fun. I wouldn't mind that. I'll go a couple of rounds with you.'

Andry looked at his dad then looked at me, sizing me up. He threw the gloves back to me along with a head guard.

'Alright, Jock. If you want?'

'Andry. I hardly think that's fair,' Mr Falconer said. 'The kid's probably never been in a fight in his life.'

Like all men, my macho pride growled deep within and I felt compelled to defend myself, regretting the words even as they left my mouth.

'Well, actually... I've been in a scrap or two. I can handle myself. Us Scots aren't pushovers. Come on, let's give it a shot.'

It was fair to say I had been in a few fights recently even if I'd never yet thrown a punch.

I made a mental effort to stop my legs shaking. My T-shirt already felt sticky with sweat. In the cooling summer evening air of the backyard Gina's dad laced my gloves up. Andry was bouncing around, throwing punches at the air. It occurred to me there was a passive aggressive undercurrent in Andry's immediate willingness to accept my challenge of combat. I had hurt his little sister. Big brothers look after their little sisters. I had no idea what I was going to do. I decided to roll the dice and go for it.

'A few times round boys then that's it,' Mr Falconer said as he lined us up opposite one another.

I stood facing this experienced, fit boxer and attempted to copy his stance; crouched, defensive, gloved arms raised to protect my head. He tapped my gloves with his and off we went. I knew I had to keep moving. That's what Mickey taught Rocky to do. Keep moving and jab occasionally. It felt like I had no strength in my arms whatsoever. These arms that could wail on the guitar and drive an audience of indie rock fans into states of euphoria, these arms were useless in the real world. They were two flimsy pieces of straw attached to my torso. Andry gave me a few soft sparring jabs, testing me out. They were swift, solid things that sent a shudder through me and pushed my body around the faded white lines of the boxing ring. Mr Falconer watched on, leaning against the kitchen door.

The air was warm and I started overheating immediately, feeling my body flush hot all over. I couldn't believe how quick Andry was. He bounced and moved back and forth with tremendous energy. I tried to punch but he wasn't there for my gloved fist to connect with. Suddenly a hail of quick jabs battered into my head and I stumbled backwards.

Fuck! This wasn't going well at all. How long was it supposed to last? There was no one watching the time. Wasn't there supposed to be a bell or something? I was already breathing heavily, my legs felt like dead weights and I was dazed by the admittedly soft punches coming my way, each one connecting with a sudden dunt and flash of white light that burst quickly across my vision like the lens flare from a film camera. Andry was going easy on me, that much was clear. I was gasping for breath when the guy landed a punch to my solar plexus that rattled through my body and sent me off my feet. He laughed out loud as my legs collapsed underneath me and my butt hit the concrete.

'I think ya might be a bit out of practice mate. I barely touched ya,' he said as he hooked an arm round mine and pulled me upright. 'I don't want to hurt you. Let's leave it there, eh?'

I was on my feet and winded but managed to say, 'Nah, I'm just getting warmed up.' Where was this bravado coming from? He looked at me as if I was deranged but shrugged his shoulders and resumed. I, too, was trying to figure out what I was doing. My mouth was writing cheques that my body was bouncing.

By this time I had begun to feel queasy and my chest was killing me. I couldn't tell if it was my pathetic lung capacity or Andry's punch that was the problem but I remained resolute about not quitting. I wanted to send a message to Gina. I wanted to let her know I'd been here and that I'd stood toe-to-toe with her brother.

We circled one another and I tried to bob and weave but only my torso responded – my legs were too heavy to move. I'd attempt a dodge and find my wooden legs planted firmly in the ground.

Andry looked pissed off at my lack of skill and boxing knowledge. He seemed to stand still for a split second and I swung wildly at him but he was gone again and two powerful taps thumped against the side of my face and I fell against the hut. I would not be deterred. I had to give a good account of myself in front of Gina's family. If I was embarrassing myself I had to find a way out of it.

Andry was shaking his head now and speaking to me as we continued circling. 'I fink you're out of puff pal. Need to get yerself back in the gym. You pop star types are too used to the big parties.'

I moved in close and tried to land one on his jaw. Before I had time to let loose with a punch he belted me hard on the side of the upper arm and the entire limb went dead. I jumped backwards and almost fell through the kitchen door but Mr Falconer steadied me.

'Persistent bugger ain't ya?' he said.

This encouraged me. I wanted them to think I was a persistent bugger. This was good. Maybe this was the way to go. Genius thinking, Joey. Get beaten up so you can display your legendary stubbornness.

My left arm felt like a dead weight but I did all I could to lift it up.

'One more then we're done,' Andry said.

This time he made a point of batting away every jab I made. I got the feeling he was mocking me. He landed one right in my stomach that sent me against the garden wall. I knew I only had a few seconds before the shock enveloped me and doubled me over so I used my left leg to spring off the side of the wall. He was looking at his dad and shrugging his shoulders and as he turned back to face me I caught him by surprise and socked him right on the nose. He stumbled backwards and I fell forwards, bending over in agony, unable to draw breath. By the time I'd regained my composure I looked up to see him coming at me again, a crooked smile on his face, shaking his head and laughing in disbelief. I remember the first punch that knocked both my arms out of the way as if they were nothing more than long grass on a woodland pathway. I don't remember the second one at all.

I could hear English voices. I was sitting down on the kitchen step. Everything faded and came into focus again. My jaw was throbbing. Mr Falconer's face was in mine, staring into my pupils.

'…Nah. You'll be alright. Drink this.'

A bottle of water was pressed in to my hand. I could hear Andry in the kitchen behind me.

'He told us he was a boxer. What was I supposed to think? Nah… Nah… it wasn't my fault. It was a cheap shot… Fuck sake… he… Alright, alright… Why? Because he's been lying here for the past five minutes and I've no idea what to do with him.'

I was still dazed and unsure what was happening when they led me out to a car and sat me in the front seat. I clung to my bottle of water.

'I don't need the hospital,' I said. 'Give me a minute.'

Andry's reply was lost in the muddle of my aching face and buzzing ears. The car was moving and I started feeling carsick immediately. The sensation went away and came back intermittently as we stopped and started, went round corners and up hills. Eventually everything began to clear up. I was in the passenger seat. Andry was driving and talking to me.

'…but I'm not gonna apologise. How was I supposed to know you were talking shit? You could've got proper hurt mate. Boxing's not a game.'

I rubbed my eyes as the stunned feeling subsided.

'Where are we going?' I asked.

'I fink you might have brain damage. That's the fourth time you've asked me that. You sure you're alright?'

'Yeah…'

'She's fucking pissed off at me now. Apparently

you've never boxed in your life? What are you? Some sort of unstoppable idiot?'

'I needed to get her attention,' I said.

I smiled into my fat lip while my aching jaw could do nothing to stop the spread of a grin. I was a genius after all. An unstoppable idiot genius.

The Last Image
by Ewan Morrison

The image of the future was already contained in the present, a forewarning, dormant, but few knew how to look for it. This image had already been taken, thousands of times, in semblances and fragments; it lay within all other images, concealed by its ubiquity. It would become the final image before it all went down and after it there would be no others.

It was a swarm of people in their thousands, each with their smart phones held above their heads, recording. They could have been fans at a concert or sporting event, or people recording a disaster or refugees filming the conditions of their internment, but there was no single spectacle which they filmed, no centre of attention: they were filming each other. Amazed and bemused at the sight of their own amassing, the mass recorded itself.

The power was down and the streets were blocked. They had come from all quarters and swarmed to the city centre looking for water, for food, for someone in authority, for reasons why and they found only each other. With no course of action, no instructions coming from above, they turned their cameras on each other. They did not realise that such an action was futile as there would be no internet to post the footage on, no news channel to sell it to, no distant relatives to send it to, no 'friends' to 'like' or 'share' it with. Who were they filming for? For their children? For God? For tech companies? For posterity? Why did they not leave and find that water, that food, that power, those questions that had not yet been formulated as to why the links had been broken. Everywhere – on motorways, in supermarkets, in malls and parks – hungry, tired, they amassed and filmed their own stupefaction. This was the final image from the era of globalisation and smart technology, the last image that would be seen by the global masses before they too passed into history and the screens went blank. An image of all we had achieved and stood for. The last recorded image from the lost age of images: an image of people taking images of people taking images.

ACKNOWLEDGMENTS

This book would not exist without the effort of a large group of people who have been generous with their talent and time. The editors would like to recognise all those whose hard work has made this book possible. We'd like to thank Zoe Strachan for her leadership, insight and wise counsel throughout this process; the University of Glasgow and its faculty for creating the opportunity for this collaboration, strengthening our curatorial and editorial skills, and granting us access to its community of writers and other resources; the Writers' Studio, New York for teaching one of the editors a lot of what she knows about writing and sharing our call for submissions with its community of talented writers; and to the writers who entrusted us with their stories. They are the heart of this anthology.

Alex Poppe, Tony Clerkson

BIOGRAPHIES

Johnny Acton's normal bag is non-fiction, though having had a crack at made-up stuff he'd like to do some more of it. A resolute non-specialist, he has written or co-authored fifteen books on subjects ranging from the role of high altitude ballooning in the early days of the space race to sausages, the origin of everyday things and the Olympics. He used to write obituaries for *The Times* and serious academic material for *Penthouse UK*. In an earlier incarnation, he was a failed soup bar magnate. He lives in Gloucestershire and keeps large black pigs.

Laura Boss is working on her first novel between bouts of international travel as a spa designer. She is currently a student at The Writers Studio and a member of Mystery Writers of America. Laura lives in Occupied San Francisco and enjoys watching urban coyotes as they track dog walkers in the The Presidio.

Syd Briscoe grew up in London with a packed bookcase and Hammer Horror movie marathons for company. She moved to Glasgow in 2009 and is currently taking an MLitt in Creative Writing at the University of Glasgow. She blames her Irish heritage for her obsession with telling stories although staying up all night writing gets her into less trouble these days. The short story *Trigger Happy* is an extract from her current novel-in-progress of the same name.

Lynsey Calderwood likes to tell stories about quirky, diverse characters who live on the fringes of society, paying homage to many misrepresented and unrepresented minority groups. She is currently working on a novel about a group of Scottish drag artists and is a volunteer writer-in-residence at Polmont Young Offenders Institution.

David Cameron made the journey from his hometown of East Kilbride to his adopted home in County Leitrim via Amsterdam. He is the author of a collection of stories, *Rousseau Moon*, and a short novel, *The Ghost of Alice Fields*. *Walking Bibi*, printed here, is an extract from his novel-in-progress, *Femke*. He has recently been shortlisted for the Hennessy Literary Awards.

John Paul Fitch is a writer who predominantly works in fiction – comics, short stories and television. He is also a published non-fiction writer, contributing articles to publications as diverse as *CQ* magazine and *Smoke and Mirrors*. Most recently, John Paul was published in 215Ink's *Ignition* anthology and in *Psychopomp Volume 4*, and last year was placed third in Ace Comics and Games national short comics. He is currently working on a collection of short horror stories. In his spare time, he raises two wild kids with his wife, in Perth, Western Australia.

Ross Garner is a professional writer from the Highlands of Scotland, currently living in Glasgow. In the past he has written local news and showbiz gossip, but he now produces online content for a management audience. In his spare time he likes to talk about writing a novel.

Gordon Legge doesn't like biographies.

Aaron Malachy Lewis was born in the Midwestern United States, and no matter where he goes, he continues to write about the Midwest. Having briefly considered a degree in biology, he earned a BA in English from a small private college in Iowa. He spent the next three years in Lawrence, Kansas, where he focused mainly on Creative Writing. After years of writing almost exclusively short pieces, he is currently working on his first novel. *Pool*, his short story printed here, is an extract from this work-in-progress. He resides in Glasgow, luckily, because he can only sleep when it rains.

Jane R Martin is a current online student in the master class at the Writers Studio in New York. When she isn't writing, Jane manages the Copeland String Quartet. Her delights are her toddler grandson, JJ, and her sheltie, Izzie. She is often seen writing on the train as she travels from Wilmington, DE to Pittsburgh to visit JJ. An essay she wrote was published in the compilation, *This I Believe: On Love*, edited by Dan Gediman, John Gregory and Mary Jo Gediman.

Charles E McGarry was born in Glasgow in 1972. He was brought up in the city and graduated with an honours degree in History and Politics from the University of Glasgow in 1994. His novel *The Road to Lisbon* was published by Birlinn-Polygon in 2012 (co-written with Martin Greig). Charles has since completed the first in his Leo Hayes series of detective novels, *The Killing of Helen Addison*. He lives in Glasgow after spells in London and Edinburgh. He has played in bands, travelled widely and loves literature, Beethoven and hillwalking. *Innocence Lost* is an extract from his novel-in-progress *The Mysterious Affair At Biggnarbriggs Hall*.

Ewan Morrison was the winner of the Scottish Book of the Year (SMIT) Fiction Prize in 2013 for his novel *Close Your Eyes*, and of the writing award of the Glenfiddich Spirit of Scotland Awards in 2012. He was the winner of the Not the Booker Prize in 2012, a finalist in the Saltire Society book of the Year 2012 and a finalist in the Creative Scotland Writer of the Year Award 2012. His first feature film, *Swung*, an adaptation of his first novel, is in production with Sigma films, directed by Colin Kennedy and starring Elena Anaya. *Swung*, published in 2005, was shortlisted for the Le Prince Maurice Award. *The Last Book You Read* and other stories led him to be short listed for the *Arena* magazine Man of the Year award in 2006.

Jack Parker is 45 years old. He lives with his family in Tucson, Arizona where he works as a general contractor. He is a member of the Writers Studio Tucson.

After listening to too many Swans albums **Graeme Rae** left home to volunteer in a Calcutta street hospital (working through middle-class guilt) then became an Edinburgh nurse (working through Christ complex) then drank his way slowly overland to SE Asia (working through nihilism) then, in Australia, studied martial arts (working through his inability to work things through) and scuba (at last – sweet mother Gaia!). He finally found a real human to talk to and promptly tricked her into marriage. With the naïve, unshakeable belief he can write his way back home he's currently studying for his MLitt in Creative Writing at Glasgow University while living, nursing and triathlon-ing in Edinburgh... when not being dark and interesting.

Marie Sanchez is a former journalist whose work has appeared in the Boston Globe and the Wall Street Journal. She is now a writer of short stories and poems and is working on a novel. She has lived in Mexico, Alaska, Paris, New York, Boston and the Bay Area in California and enjoys scuba diving, running and martial arts.

Kev Sherry is a musician and songwriter in Scottish indie band Attic Lights (Island Records/Elefant Records.) He has collaborated with Cerys Matthews, The Vaselines, Echo and The Bunnymen and Camera Obscura and performed on stage with Travis, Cerys Matthews, Camera Obscura, The Fratellis, Frightened Rabbit and Paul Heaton. He is an occasional music journalist for STV and is recording his debut solo album, intended as a companion piece to his first novel, *Twenty Ways To Live Creatively* from which *Split Decision* is an extract.

Marcelle Thiébaux has stories in *Literal Latté*, *Karamu*, *The Cream City Review*, *Grand Central Noir*, *Urban Fantasy (KY Story)*, and *Akashic Books Mondays are Murder*. She's the author of a 13th century novel, *Unruly Princess*. Forthcoming in paperback is *The Stag of Love* on the medieval love chase. She lives in New York.

6140372R00077

Printed in Great Britain
by Amazon.co.uk, Ltd.,
Marston Gate.